HANGOVER SOUP

ALSO BY LOUISE REDD   **Playing the Bones**

HANGOVER SOUP

A NOVEL

LOUISE REDD

LITTLE, BROWN AND COMPANY
Boston   New York   London

FIRST EDITION

The characters and events in this book are fictitious. Any similarity to real persons, living or dead, is coincidental and not intended by the author.

Library of Congress Cataloging-in-Publication Data
Redd, Louise.
    Hangover soup : a novel/by Louise Redd. — 1st ed.
        p.   cm.
    ISBN 0-316-47900-4 (hc)
    I. Title.
    PS3568.E296H36   1999
    813'.54 — dc21   99-18936

10 9 8 7 6 5 4 3 2 1

MV-NY

Printed in the United States of America

For Matthew

ACKNOWLEDGMENTS

I owe a great debt to the following people: to Leigh Hopper, Tim Kreider, Karla Kuban, Joe McDade, Dave Feller-Kopman, and Michelle Feller-Kopman, for reading my early drafts; to Ginger Barber, my agent and a great source of support; to Sarah Burnes, my wonderful editor, whose careful work helped bring this one to life; to my friend Tom Wissemann for telling me stories and talking to me about tomatoes; to my sisters-in-law, Martha McEvoy Fjermedal and Mary Kay Connors, for their particular support; to my friend Amy Peters for loaning me the name of her fabulous radio show, *Revel Without a Pause,* which in real life is broadcast on KOTO from Telluride, Colorado; to my parents, Lady Margaret and True Redd, for giving me 811 Kinney Avenue, where much of this book was written; to Dar Craft for indispensable support; to Isabel Feller-Kopman, my precious godchild, for daily inspiration; to Rule Brand and Michael Pietsch for giving me a start; to Aimee and Allan Redd, Nicole Austin, Andrew Cohen, Patrick Woodall, Lee Gaillard, Kat Reeves, and the Evans family for essential encouragement; and to Matthew McEvoy, my husband, for everything.

PART I

"Don't cut my throat. I may
want to do that myself later."

— *Casey Stengel, to his barber*

Save the Ales

If Jay were telling this story, he might start it after the wreck, after his life changed forever and mine did too. But it's me telling it, and I'm going to start it before. There are things that came before that can't be forgotten, things that even the splintering of glass and metal and a person's bones can't block out. I'm going to start by saying this: I met my husband in college, where it's hard to tell who's a true alcoholic and who's not. It's not an excuse, but I think it should be mentioned.

It should be mentioned that for the first year of our marriage I thought drinking was something we did with dinner. I thought of the bottles of wine the same way I thought of the candles on the table, or the love notes Jay sometimes slipped into my fortune cookie — if it was a fortune-cookie sort of dinner — the notes that read, "Look at the man sitting across the table from you and know that he loves you very much." It took me a while to realize that for Jay the wine was the nourishment, the romance, the reason for having dinner in the first place. I was slow to catch on to the affair between Jay and the bottle. I realized at a late hour that I was just a chaperone, that the fortune-cookie love notes were a toll Jay paid on the way to his high. Or maybe that's wrong; maybe I knew all along. Darrah, my best friend, once said to me in frustration, "Didn't the 'Save the Ales' sticker on his car tip you off?"

After I knew, I wanted one thing in life: I wanted Jay to love me more than he loved booze. I wanted him to look at his bottle of gin and say something like, "Oh, this bugs you? It's gone." Then toss it over his shoulder like a handful of salt. I can barely remember what I wanted before I knew. I think I wanted to be a great teacher, to inspire my athletes (or "student-athletes," as I was contractually bound to call them) to do better than they needed to. I wanted to send them off to the NFL and the major and minor leagues and their assistant coaching positions with something in their brains besides curveballs and zone defenses.

After I knew, in the second year of our marriage, I stopped drinking with Jay. I even stopped cooking with wine. I went a whole winter without making my favorite shiitake mushroom cream sauce because the mushrooms need to be soaked in one and a third cups medium-dry white wine. I tried once making it without the wine, but it wasn't the same sauce.

Shortly after our third anniversary, I stopped making my hangover soup, my top-secret, garlic-laden recipe capable of curing the most vicious hangover. I let my husband suffer, let him feel his brain was a shrunken, dried thing rattling in his skull.

In the fourth year of our marriage I took up running, thinking I could outrace my anger at Jay for being a drunk, at myself for having married a drunk, at all the various things in Texas that seemed to support drunkenness, like the

billboard near the turnoff to our house that read FROM HERE
TO THERE IS TOO FAR WITHOUT A SIX-PACK. On a bad
night I lobbed a rock at the billboard, but it didn't even
make a mark.

Near the beginning of the fifth year I stopped listening to
Jay's radio show, *Revel Without a Pause,* broadcast six nights
a week from KXAL. Jay always took a small cooler of beer to
work. He always took some pot and his little metal bat (I
know these words, *bat, bong, kif,* although I wouldn't mind
forgetting them). On certain nights he encouraged his listeners to call in with their personal hangover remedies, which
he carefully recorded in a black spiral notebook. He had am-
bitions of compiling the cures into a book, which he planned
to call *How to Get the Hangover Over.* I stopped listening because I could tell from Jay's voice and his song list exactly
what substances, and in what quantities, he'd ingested.
Straight-up jazz meant three beers and half a joint. Coltrane's
weirder stuff meant the rest of the joint. Grateful Dead
meant he'd finished the six-pack. Billie Holiday meant gin.

On Jay's night off, we tried different things: We pretended a culinary interest in wine; we said Jay was drinking
gin and tonics because the weather was warm, because a gin
and tonic is such a nice warm-weather drink; we pretended
he would be just fine without any of it. I personally tried
imagining I was European, that I had been raised in some
lovely French village where four-year-olds hold glasses of
watered-down wine in their fat little fingers. I occasionally
pretended we were in the middle of Prohibition, that I had
a closetful of intricately beaded flapper dresses, that Jay
drank in romantic rebellion against our oppressive gov-
ernment. Other nights I simply nagged, cried, begged, and

yelled. Sometimes I offered what seemed like a rational argument: "Why do you need a central nervous system depressant when we have hundred-degree heat right outside our door? You could not drink and we could just turn off the air conditioner."

"Spoken like a Texan," he'd say with a lift of his glass and a smile so dazzling I'd momentarily lose my grip on my complaints. "I love the way *y'all* turn the heat into a selling point."

"You drunken Yankee," I'd say, wishing we were not already at that point in the evening when Jay's face began to lose its structure, when forming a sentence and a smile required incredible effort and a long period of rest afterward. I wanted to take my hands and sculpt the skin back tightly over his bones. I wanted to jerk his eyelids up from their half-closed laziness and paint an intelligent, alert look across his eyes. I wanted to shape his mouth into a form suitable for conversation, or kissing. But I kept my hands in my pockets and let Jay continue on his own.

On the nights when it was finally clear that Jay's interest in a gigantic quantity of a certain wine had nothing to do with the way said wine brought out the fruity undertones of a citrus-glazed salmon fillet, when it was obvious that the gin and tonics had nothing to do with either the warm weather or my imagined French heritage, Jay would shut himself up in our bedroom with the bottle of gin and stacks of CDs. Voices not my husband's boomed out at me: Aretha Franklin, Lightning Hopkins, James Brown proclaiming himself a sex machine. Occasionally, at the urging of these beloved voices, Jay wrote me long letters and left them on my pillow, where I'd find them next to his unconscious self.

I'm a fool for Jay's letters. They said things like this: "You were beautiful the first time you smiled at me. We were sitting across from each other in the crowded history seminar room, and you looked smart and busy. Through your preoccupation you smiled at me and I felt a thrill I can never adequately put into words. You made me look twice at the twilight streaming through the chains over the windows. I felt an immense urge, but one in which the sexual was joined by something else entirely. It felt unrealistic at the time."

Often such a letter would move me to strip off his clothes and kiss the length of his body, starting at one end or the other and working my way slowly up or down his long, cold, weighted limbs. When I'd finished every inch of one side — usually the front, because he almost always passed out on his back, which is supposed to be dangerous, in the Jimi Hendrix kind of way — I'd roll him over and do the other side, kissing until my lips were stretched and dry, until my face heated with effort. I'd cover Jay's body with mine, trying to warm it, trying to contact every inch of exposed skin. I'd shimmy down his length until the tops of my feet covered the tops of his feet, until my hipbones rocked into his upper thighs, until my face filled the space between his ribs. I'd spread my hair, of which I have a generous helping, so thickly over Jay's face that he'd stir slightly, trying to find a breath. Then I'd thin the layer of blondness out over the pillows, across Jay's pillow to the edge of my own, where that evening's letter rested.

Another one read: "Faith Anne Abbott Evers, I feel as though our time together has been just the smallest prelude to a life which can't help but grow, and to a love which can only increase. Your face for me has the power and grace of dawn. I love you so much, Faith, my Faith Anne. I'll never have words for it — thank God you have so many names."

When I'd finished reading that particular letter, I stripped off my clothes and stretched out next to Jay on the bedspread. I took his arm with the floppy hand attached to it and ran the palm of the hand over the curve of my belly, up the quick incline of my hipbones. I steered the hand over one breast, then the other. The fingers slept against my curves. I dragged the hand back down past my waist and gathered two of the fingers, two strips of that cold, fleshy sandpaper. I pinned them together, then dipped them into the folds of the deepest part of me, the part my mother calls "the most sacred room of your body." I didn't feel particularly sacred. I coaxed Jay's slumping, unconscious fingers inside me, warming them. I pressed them here and there, Jay's now moist fingers, until I felt his call ringing through my body.

This was winter, a dry winter, one without a single rain. Every Saturday morning while Jay was still unconscious, I drove over to Darrah's and watered the peach tree I had planted the day her daughter, Lucy, was born. Darrah was the medical reporter for our daily newspaper and had spent her entire pregnancy waving foreboding articles in my face, consumed with worry about twisted umbilical cords and twelve-toed babies. Darrah is twisted a few turns too tight herself. Lucy was perfect, as it happened, my favorite part of her the almost-invisible little eyebrows that tented up over her dark blue eyes. I'd wanted to do something to commemorate the birth, to give the baby something that would grow along with her. Each Saturday I soaked the little tree with the mixture my mother had taught me to use: seaweed, fish emulsion, molasses.

Finally it came to this: a letter that ended, "I love you, Faith Anne. I wish I could say something more substantial, something that really delivered the feeling that hurts my throat and my heart and heats my gut every time I think of your face." That one made me kneel, one knee on either side of Jay's head, hoping my scent would wake him from his stupor. It was too awkward to hold his sluggish lips with my hands against my larger, more fragrant lips, against the part of me that Jay, in one of his drunken letters, had called my "other mouth." I used the bridge of his nose instead. His forehead. The grit of his unshaven cheek. Then I caught my reflection in our bedroom window: me squatting over the face of my unconscious husband. A fierce energy looped through my body; I had nowhere to put it. In the glossy, dark rectangle of the window, I looked like a woman urinating in the woods near a large, rotted log.

I went to the bathroom for a washcloth and soap and wiped my scent from Jay's face. I sat next to him on the bed until the room grew light, then lighter, until the bright Texas spring sun blazed through the open window, until mosquitoes drifted in and drew high-alcohol-content blood from my husband and drifted out again, gorged. I watched Jay's dark brown hair, hair with the slight but determined curves of a leaf. I watched his good high cheekbones and the faint lines on either side of his mouth that deepened into dimples when he smiled. I watched him so long I saw the thickening of his beard, the stubble blooming on his chin. I read that night's letter over and over, and I told myself that even though Jay loved me more than some women are ever loved, he still loved alcohol an increment more. I told myself that if alcohol were a woman, Jay wouldn't be able to keep his hands off her. If alcohol were a woman, she'd have some tacky, tropical name: Desirée, or Racquel. If alcohol were a woman, she and I would have tried to become friends, and failed.

I sat next to Jay's naked body, watching his skin mist with cool, gin-scented sweat, until he drew an arm over his eyes, until he coordinated his brain and tongue to grind out the words, "Faith, the shades? Bright in here."

It was barely March. The sun was bright but still a spring sun. It wasn't yet a weapon, an enemy, something to hide from. Darrah's little girl was almost two months old and her peach tree shimmered with juicy green leaves no longer than an eyelash. Darrah had grown an entire baby while Jay had been drunk, while I'd spent hour after dark hour striking my body against his, as if we were two pieces of flint, as if I could make a spark.

I closed the shades. Jay's face relaxed. Then I thought again about our house, which we'd bought only two years before, about our jobs, which required drastically different levels of sobriety. Jay was in his fifth year of working as a disc jockey and often went to work stoned, spewing out the long, funny monologues that had become his trademark. I spent my days imploring athletes to stay straight, to study hard, to listen to their mamas and get those degrees. I spoke daily of the Game of Life, conjuring strained comparisons to the games of football and baseball.

I thought briefly about Jay's body in a substance-free moment, Jay's body alive and in deep conversation with my own body, then I brought back the reflection of myself squatting over the rotted log that was my husband and said, "Jay, I've had enough. I need to try something else."

"Faith," Jay groaned from beneath the arm that draped his face. "Jesus, can we talk about it later." His voice scraped out of his throat, dry and thin. I was tempted to water him, as one waters a plant. I was tempted to mix up the seaweed/fish emulsion/molasses combination and drench him with it.

"It *is* later," I said. "You've been drunk every day for as long as I can remember. When's the last time we made love, Jay? If my vagina were a child, they'd take it away from you and put it in foster care!"

Jay started laughing, then stopped with a shudder of pain. "Faith," Jay said, still from beneath his arm, "don't you love me? Come on, Buddy."

"I love you when you're not drinking," I said. "I'm crazy about you when you're not drinking." This was not entirely true. I loved Jay all the time. I could feel traces of love in my blood even when he was stupid-drunk. But I could also feel it destroying us, and I was willing to take the gamble that my leaving would wake him up.

I waited for him to say something else, then realized he'd fallen asleep again. His arm slipped from his eyes to his chest.

"What the hell, Jay?" I said. "You're Mr. Articulate when it's time to spew a bunch of stoned bullshit over the radio but when it comes to losing your wife you can't think of anything to say?"

I would not stay long enough to act out the rest of our script: Jay sleeping away the morning, then shaking off his hangover with a shower and a joint, then a burst of apologies and promises not to drink that day. "How about an alcohol-free day, Buddy?" he would say, as if he were offering me a plate of something delicious. After a particularly bad night, he'd lure me with talk of a week, or even a month of sobriety. It didn't really matter; his promises had the life span of a paper towel. I twisted off my wedding ring and set it on the night table, although I could hardly stand to let go of it, although I wanted to snatch it back and jam it onto my finger.

"Well, I have something to say," I told him. "If you can't quit drinking, you're no longer going to be married to me. Just think about whether you want to quit or not," I said. "Just let me know, okay?" I leaned over until my mouth touched his ear. "Okay?" I yelled.

"Right!" he yelled back, eyes jolting open and then sinking closed.

"Don't strain yourself, Jay," I said as I gathered clothes and books and CDs in my arms. "It's okay if our last conversation consists entirely of monosyllables."

I walked outside and threw my armful of stuff through the open rear window of my car. I ran back inside for another load. "You drunk, me gone!" I yelled from the kitchen as I pulled dishes out of the cabinets. I flung them into the car, hoping they would break. I tossed in my recipe box, but not before I pulled out the recipe for hangover soup and tore it into a hundred tiny pieces. When the car was almost full, I threw in Jay's letters, but rolled up the windows so they couldn't blow away.

I went back into the bedroom and dragged up one of Jay's eyelids. I wanted to see the color of his eyes one more time before I left: green, the light green of new growth on a plant.

They're at their greenest when the whites of his eyes are bloodshot, as they were, of course, that morning.

I released the lid of his eye. He didn't seem to notice. On my way out I picked up Jay's stupid black spiral notebook full of hangover cures and hurled it into the car.

My car felt weighted and strange, on the drive across town to the university. I would ask Coach Talwen, my boss, to give me a room in the dorms. In exchange, I would offer to be on call for the student-athletes twenty-four hours a day. Football season was over, but baseball season was on, and we were all supposed to be busy redeeming ourselves from our miserable 23–33 record of the season before. Coach had signed five promising young players, two already with junior college experience. We were supposed to be great this year. We were supposed to have a chance. I felt certain Coach Talwen would agree to my plan, and I concentrated on not crying until it was done and I was alone in my dorm room. I bit my lip, held my breath, to let my body know I needed it to behave for just an hour or so longer.

My car's engine stalled on the little hill at Fifth and Lamar and I almost rolled back into a looming Suburban. At the Twelfth Street light a boy with rainbow-colored dreads wanted to hand me a flier about something, but I couldn't get the window rolled down, which happens sometimes, and had to communicate this to him through shrugging and desperate window-rolling motions. He finally stuck the flier under my windshield wiper and flashed me a peace sign as he walked away.

It wasn't a hot day, but as soon as I knew the window wouldn't go down, I felt like I was crossing the Sahara instead of Austin, Texas. I thought if I didn't get a breath of cool air, I might pass out and cross over into the oncoming lane and annihilate someone with my 1966 Chevelle, a heavy car on any day but on this particular day fortified with my entire wardrobe and my bone china and some of the everyday china and most of the classics of modern literature and Jay's own personal written-in-cursive words of love. At the last light before I turned onto campus, my hands were shaking against the steering wheel and I couldn't remember whether red meant stop, or go.

Texas Woman

After two long weeks of dorm life, Jay still had not called up with a stunning array of apologies and promises not to drink. Instead he had sent me postcards, care of the athletic department, covered in words that meant something to me: bits of my favorite poems, the lyrics of songs we'd made out to, the career stats of my favorite professional baseball player. I analyzed the postcards relentlessly, hoping I might discover, if I read the message backward or upside down, a clearly stated intention to get sober.

For two weeks I didn't listen to Jay's show, though I longed to hear his voice. I spent my evenings in the study lounge, harassing my ballplayers, trying to convince them that they might someday be judged on something other than their batting averages. I spent long hours pounding Spanish vocabulary into the sullen head of Micah Levin, the ace of our pitching staff. Based solely on his suspicion that the professor was a lesbian, Micah had given up all hope of passing the class.

"She ain't gonna pass me," he told me one night, his huge lap covered in vocabulary lists. Micah spoke at a grudgingly slow pace. "She's a carpet muncher, Miss Evers."

"You think you can't get a fair call from an umpire just because he doesn't want to get in your pants, doll?"

"That's different," he said.

"How?"

"Just different." He started drawing elaborate sun rays emanating from the holes in his notebook paper. My athletes are, in general, world-class doodlers.

I wondered how Micah would ever pass that Spanish class when he could barely express himself in his mother tongue, but I told him he could do it, I told him Spanish was a good language to know. "What if you end up on a pitching staff with the next Fernando Valenzuela? Don't you want to be able to have at least a primitive conversation? You know, 'Good pitch,' 'That ump's blind,' 'Let's go count our millions.'"

He abandoned the sun rays and started rearranging his tiny dreadlocks so they weighted one side of his head. "Who?" he said. Micah had a hard time cranking out a syllable like *who* and playing with his hair simultaneously, thus the delay.

"Hey, no need to know anything about the history of the game you play every single day. No big deal."

Micah sighed. "What's your point, Miss Evers?"

Usually I had a world of patience for my boys, but Jay had used up his own portion and most of theirs too.

"My point is I'm through for tonight. You're a big boy; you can go over these verbs yourself. My point is I have something better to do."

I threw my books into my bag and walked down the hall to my room. My so-called something better was this: I clicked on the radio. I slid the dial slowly, as if I were undressing for someone, as if each movement of the bright pink indicator stripped away another piece of clothing, until its arrival in the upper nineties left me completely bared.

Taj Mahal, with the Pointer Sisters trailing a lazy chant behind him, finished singing "Texas Woman" before Jay's voice made my heart seize up, made me touch my jeans and T-shirt to make certain I was still clothed.

"I had a Texas woman," Jay said, in his husky, low, I'm-baked-and-don't-you-know-it voice. "I did indeed. A fine, fine, Texas woman, like the man said, a woman to satisfy my very soul. A woman who stayed with me through the bad times, who kept my name on her lips when she had no reason to speak it, a woman with legs so long they bring basketball to mind. A woman who wears sneakers with dresses, who sings while she makes sandwiches. A woman whose hair is so amazingly blond that women stop her in the grocery store and inquire, 'What kind of shampoo do you use?' A woman who once described Sarah Vaughan's voice as 'dessert.' As in rich, rare, more addictive than chocolate. Here's the Great One with Ray Brown on bass, Joe Pass on guitar, Oscar Peterson on piano, and Louis Bellson on drums, singing 'How Long Has This Been Going On?'"

Both voices, Sarah Vaughan's and Jay's, prodded deeply at my heart. Sarah's voice had always meant making love with Jay, and Jay's voice had sometimes meant making love with Jay but sometimes meant he was saying something I didn't much want to hear, something like, "Beer is food." I wondered if giving up my wonderful sober moments with Jay was worth being rid of the drunken ones. I wondered what I would do if my gamble didn't pay off. I told myself something I frequently told my ballplayers: *Failure is a big part of the game, dear ones. The men who fail six times out of ten are baseball's greatest heroes.*

I turned off the radio and the song kept going in my head until Cory Bell, the Longhorns' second baseman, rapped on my door. He needed help with a personal essay, due the next morning. As he spoke, he rubbed a hand over the top of his blond crew cut into which he had shaved 7, his uniform number. He rubbed as if to elicit my help, as if I were a genie he could coax into service.

"Cory, it's ten thirty," I told him in my most motherly voice. "Why didn't you start working on this earlier? Do you wait until ten thirty the night before a big game to start thinking about it?" I tried to focus on my mini-lecture in spite of Cory's distracting T-shirt: an incredibly muscular Jesus Christ on a cross, a cross made from some highly polished, not very biblical-looking material, topped by the words "His Pain, Your Gain."

"I got a title," Cory offered. He held up a smudged piece of notebook paper with the words "My Walk with the Lord" penciled across the top. "What do you think, Miss Evers? Am I winning the Game of Life or what?" Most of my ballplayers called me "Miss Evers" or "Mizevers," too lazy to speak the more complicated "Mrs." I let them.

"You're in there," I said. "Let's go out to the study room." I regretted having turned on Jay's show; I suddenly wanted to get away from the radio, my single bed, and Jay's black spiral notebook, which contained things like this: "Hangover Cure #16, called in by a self-described 'faithful listener' in South Austin: 'Cabbage soaked in Kool-Aid, man. You'll be able to go to work and everything.'"

"I'm into this thing about you being on call all the time,"

Cory said as we walked down the noisy hallway. "I think I'm gonna do okay this semester."

"I think you are too," I said in the bright, my-heart-is-not-broken voice I'd been practicing.

How could Jay call me a fine Texas woman without his heart shattering into a hundred jagged pieces? How could he even listen to that song, the song that had been our anthem during the period of our lives when I still drank with Jay, when it took buckets of alcohol to overtake the drunkenness we felt for each other anyway? I focused on Jesus Christ, buff and miserable on Cory's T-shirt, and tried to replace Jay's voice with the noises of the hallway: the fiercely competing boom boxes, the ESPN *SportsCenter* theme song, weight-lifting grunts from the open doorway of Leo Rhodes's room. Because the NCAA had outlawed athletic dorms, some of the rooms we passed were occupied by tiny, pale physics majors, or English majors who were so horrified by my illiterate darlings that they never opened their doors. Coach and I were always brainstorming about ways to get around the NCAA rule; one of our favorite fantasies involved convincing a wealthy alum to buy an off-campus apartment building big enough to house at least our first-stringers. Anne, my staffer who tutored basketball players and nonstarters, had a theory I liked: She thought universities should do away with the pretense that athletes were also students and simply hire teams to represent them.

"Hey!" I said as we passed Mike Winston, who had hit a home run to win that day's game and whose ego was horribly inflamed in spite of the fact that he owned what I privately thought of as the World's Ugliest Goatee. "Aren't you supposed to be reading *Anna Karenina*?"

Mike informed me, through a mouthful of microwave popcorn and a slow Alabama accent, that he didn't really need to read it; one of the outfielders had already told him the plot.

"Miss Evers —" Cory said.

"Hold on, Cory. Well," I said to Mike, "spill it."

"Anna goes out on a date with some dude and gets smacked by a train."

"Meet me in the study lounge in twenty minutes," I said, and he walked away stroking his goatee with buttery fingers and muttering about how he was just going to rent the video, fuck this *book* shit.

"Miss Evers," Cory said, "I'm kinda into this essay. I got a couple ideas for it already."

"That's great, sweetie. Hold on," I said as we reached Micah's open door. He had his TV cranking, Orioles vs. Yankees, so loud he couldn't hear my initial nagging. He slurped down the last of his Big Gulp, tossed the empty cup onto his trash pile, and turned the volume down some.

"Yeah?" he said.

"Don't you think you should be going over those verbs again?"

"Nah," he said, staring at the TV. The Orioles' second baseman zipped a quick grounder up the third-base line for a single. "Mr. Six Million Dollars a Year," Micah said.

"Honey, don't watch the dollars," I told him for the hundredth time. "Watch the game."

"Miss Evers," Cory said. "What about my walk with the Lord?"

"Hold on, Cory. Mic, you don't want to miss the Houston trip."

"Wouldn't mind."

"How can you say that? You're having a great year on the field. There's no reason you can't have a great year in the classroom as well." Whenever I talked to my boys like that, I felt like I ought to be shaking pom-poms and leaping around in a very short, pleated skirt. But still I kept talking, kept cheering, while Micah shrugged and turned up the volume again.

"Miss Evers," Cory said. He rubbed his 7 in frustration. He let his jaw hang slack, drawing loud skeins of air through his mouth.

"Cory," I said, "breathe through your nose, honey. The oxygen will get to your brain faster that way. And you, Micah Levin, you find your vocabulary list and meet me in the study lounge. Half the world speaks Spanish and there's no reason why you can't speak it as well."

Micah sighed and punched the Mute button to quiet the TV.

"You're a pain in the ass, Miss Evers," he said, his gaze caught in the snare of a Nike commercial.

"That's my job," I said. "I'll see you in a few."

"Miss Evers," Cory said.

"Okay, doll, we're walking now," I said as we headed down the hall. "You, me, and the Lord, doing a power walk, all right?"

"All right," he said, giving the 7 a final stroke.

Cory Bell may have been enjoying a pleasant walk with the Lord that semester, but he was also executing blurry, humiliating steals on every pitcher the Longhorns faced. Keeping him eligible for play was one of the more important aspects of my job, and I felt grateful to Cory, his Lord, the rabid UT alums whose contributions paid my salary, the game of baseball, and any other deserving parties for smoothing Jay from my mind for a precious few minutes. A moment without thinking about Jay was like being underwater: silent and peaceful, lovely and brief.

By the time Cory and I had adequately described his walk with the Lord (the daily prayers, the leadership of pregame Bible studies, the quest to constantly sport a T-shirt featuring a clear, concise message from You Know Who), by the time I'd badgered Mike Winston into reading twenty whole pages of *Anna Karenina*, by the time I'd harassed Micah to the point where he threw his vocabulary list on the floor of the study lounge and yelled, "I wish you'd get back with your man and quit riding my ass so hard!" it was after one A.M. and Jay's *Revel Without a Pause* had given way to *Just Jazz*. As I slid into my single bed and clicked off the bolted-to-the-night-table lamp, the host of the show was talking about Thelonious Monk's contribution to bebop. The deejay's voice didn't stir a thing in me, and I knew I'd be able to sleep.

A Woman

In the early mornings of my dorm life, before my ballplayers were alert enough to need me, I started tuning the radio to Jay's archenemy, to his primary competition at KXAL, a woman who called herself the Mistress of Morals. From six-thirty to ten-thirty A.M., with brief breaks for traffic updates, the Mistress answered calls from people walking a thin moral line, and with searing common sense she shoved them to the side of good and right.

"Your son's a bum," she'd tell someone who needed to kick out an errant adult child. "And when you harbor a bum you know what that makes you?" The Mistress boiled everything down to some sort of bumdom: bum marriages, bum attitudes, bum parenting, bum pregnancies, bum sexuality.

"A bum?" came the tremulous answer from the mother whose twenty-five-year-old son continued to spend his days eating Cheerios and watching music videos when he had a perfectly good college degree, the son who wouldn't set foot in his father's boilerplate manufacturing company even though there was a job there waiting for him on a big, fat, engraved silver platter, but no, he didn't want to get off his be-hind and go down to the factory to investigate life as an adult working person, didn't want to have so much as a look-see.

I quickly noticed that a large proportion of the Mistress's callers were partial to the term *look-see*. When I was tempted, each night, to turn on Jay's show, I'd say out loud, "Get yerself down to the study lounge to have a look-see at them boys." I had given in that once, the night Jay called me a fine Texas woman, but not again.

Sometimes I thought about phoning the Mistress myself, calling her up to whine, "My husband's an alcoholic! What should I do?" But instead I simply imagined what she would say, imagined myself either taking her advice or blatantly, foolishly ignoring it. Both options amused me; each was comforting in its own way. When it was time to call my mother, to tell her Jay and I had separated, I imagined the Mistress asking one of her favorite questions, the one she used to boot her callers from their procrastinating sloth: "When you look in the mirror tomorrow morning, do you want to see a woman or do you want to see a little girl?"

Although I thought it might be fun to look in the mirror and see a little girl, the girl I once was with two blond braids and a mist of freckles, I picked up the phone and began to dial, mouthing the only answer that would be acceptable to the Mistress: *a woman*.

"Sugar!" Mother said when she heard my voice. "Guess what I'm doing?"

"Mother, I need to talk to you about something." I stretched out on my institutional bed, my bed with no dents, slants, lumps, or features of interest. My bed with no history. I horrified myself by reaching under my skirt and into my panties and stroking myself with great concentration.

"Just guess, honey," Mother said, and I jerked my hand away, as if she could see me.

I took an educated guess based on everything I know about my mother. "You're growing some new tomato variety and it's going to solve world hunger."

"No, Sugar, but you're in the ballpark. I'm trying to break the world's record for largest tomato. Heaviest, that is, not tallest. Anyone can grow a tall plant. It's getting the fruit to a decent size without its cracking that's the hard part."

"I'm sure you'll win, Mother."

"Well, some man in Oklahoma has the record right now. But Texas should have it, don't you think? Texas is *bigger* than Oklahoma. Texas is bigger than France!" Sometimes when Mother talks I listen more to her southern accent than to what she's actually saying. She grew up in Mississippi and all her words are soft and flexible, available to take on as many syllables as she feels like giving them. I focused on the way *France* had suddenly become *Fray-untz*.

"Mother," I said, wishing I could add enough syllables to postpone indefinitely what I had to tell her, "Jay and I are separated. I left him a couple of weeks ago. I don't know what will happen." I imagined what fun it would be to call up my mother with some good news: My ballplayers are making straight A's; Jay's been given a raise; I'm having a baby.

"What on Earth, Faith?"

"Jay has a drinking problem and we haven't been able to resolve it. He hasn't been able to cut down or quit and I haven't been able to accept him as he is."

"Sugar, you never said a word."

"I know." I'd never said a word to anyone except Darrah,

and Jay himself, of course. And my pillow. And the interior of my car. And Grace, our cat. Jay and I had been watching a Cubs game, early in our life together, the day the cat had wandered up onto Jay's porch, skinny and in obvious need of a home. We'd decided to name him after whoever turned out to be the hero of the game, which, luckily, was the well-named first baseman Mark Grace. His name could have been Ryno, Dawson, Dunston.

"Well, honey," Mother said, "is he just knee-walking drunk every day?"

"No. Some days. Hold on, Mother, someone's knocking on my door."

It was Tommy Cox, our scrappy little left fielder who was what I called a metal head; he survived solely on the advantage that college hitters have of using an aluminum bat. "Miss Evers," he said, "I got a quiz on *King Lear* tomorrow and the video store's out of it and I can't find the *Cliff's Notes* either. You gotta help me."

"Tommy, I know this may sound radical, but do you have a copy of the actual play?"

"Um, yeah."

"Go to your room, turn off the TV, turn off the stereo, sit down, and start reading, and I'll be there as soon as I finish talking to my mother."

"Okay. Okay, I'll see you in a few, right?" I closed the door. "Sorry, Mother."

"That's all right. Now, honey, has he hit you?"

"No."

"And you don't think you can live with it?"

"No, I don't."

"Well, maybe he'll make some changes. Listen, baby, I'm sorry, but I've got to run. Can we talk later?"

"Send me your column this week?" Mother, under the pen name of the Tomato Lady, wrote a weekly gardening column for the Houston paper.

"Oh, I will. It's about how to start tomatoes from seed."

Then we hung up, as usual, without Mother having said one single thing I wanted her to say. I wanted to write up a vocabulary list for her, to coach her on the proper words and phrases the way I coached Micah.

I love you, sweetheart, she could have said.

It's not your fault, honey, would have been fine too.

Is there anything I can do to help? might have been nice.

Well, I'll just let these tomato plants die of heatstroke while I zip right over to Austin to comfort you, Sugar, would have been just about perfect.

Mother drove me crazy the same way my smartest ballplayers did. Just as I knew they were capable of academic excellence, I knew Mother had it in her to love me the way she loved her tomatoes; I had seen glimmers of it in the past, in moments when I was sick or sad, in the breaks between growing seasons. But it would be difficult to compete with the World's Largest Tomato, no matter how extensive my problems.

We'd also hung up without any mention of the other alcoholic in our lives: Daddy. There's not much to say about Daddy. He doesn't do anything horrible. He's just not really there. He's an intelligent man, a successful man, but the kind of father who responded to his child's asking, "Daddy, why is the sky blue?" by saying, as he strode quickly past with a drink, "The blue wavelengths in white sunlight are scattered by tiny particles floating in the atmosphere, Faith." End of discussion. No room for "But, Daddy, what are particles?" No time to take me on his lap and discuss the intricacies of the sky. When I have my own child, I'm going to tell her wild stories about birds of prey painting the sky blue with luminous, dripping brushes, with swooping, disorganized strokes. There's more than enough time in this life for reality.

If I had mentioned my father, Mother would have said that Daddy works hard at the hospital stitching up all those cut-up, shot-up people; that he deserves to have a drink when he gets home from work, a drink or four or five. She would have called his drinks, in her charming southern accent, "highballs." She would have told me a person's not an alcoholic until he's stumbling around jobless in dirty, torn clothes, until he's *knee-walking drunk* every day. She might have reminded me that it all comes out in the wash. "It all comes out in the wash" has always been one of her favorite expressions. I think of it often when I do laundry, when a stain not only does not come out but seems to become more stubbornly entrenched, when a drop of blood or a smear of chocolate becomes a permanent part of the fabric. *It does* not *all come out in the wash*, I think.

Mother could afford not to care how much Daddy drank because she had something she loved more than people: her garden. She didn't spend her days, as I did, jumping through mental hoops to try to justify staying in her marriage. Some days I thought of Jay's drinking as something outside of both of us, as a dark force jerking Jay around like a strung puppet, jolting the glass of gin from the table to his mouth, back and forth, again and again. Some days I thought of it as something we had to fight together, as something that had to be beaten back, like mosquitoes or a vicious dog. But most days I thought of it as a choice Jay made, a lazy, bad choice like turning on the TV instead of picking up a book, a choice he made repeatedly and for which I could clearly blame him.

If I had had something I loved the way Mother loved her garden, maybe I would have been happy to mix one gin and tonic after another for my husband. I did, and do, have other things I love intensely: baseball, jazz, Darrah and Lucy, watching the fog in a student's eyes clear as he starts to understand something. But I loved Jay best of everything in this world, and I wanted him to love me best as well.

Sometimes We Had Fun

The morning after I'd told Mother about the separation, I woke up furious about her underwhelming show of support. I thought about how long it had taken me to get angry at Jay, to finally say *enough*, and I wondered how much longer I would stand for being ignored by my own mother. It had been only, oh, twenty-nine years. I'd give her another couple of chances. Determined to calm down, I walked over to the west campus early yoga class, where I bent myself into one posture after another, stretching away any trace of fury.

Gisela, the instructor, patrolled the room in her purple leotard, on the lookout for rounded spines, collapsed inner ankles. I had no idea what a collapsed inner ankle was, but I loved to hear Gisela say in her weighty German accent, "We do not collapse the inner ankle, *ever!*" I kept my ankles sturdy, my spine straight in my best version of the Downward-Facing Dog.

"Open the back of the knee," Gisela said. "Lift the sitting bones *high*. This pose is not about hanging *out*," she said. "It is about *work*." I stretched, expanded, lifted, did everything I could think of to avoid the dreaded hanging-out. I began to confuse Gisela with the Mistress. I feared momentarily that Gisela would label my not completely open backs of the knees those of a bum.

Although I was supposed to keep my neck *long,* although Gisela said, "If you want to crick your neck, save that for some *other* day," I turned my neck just enough to look at the other women in the class. The woman closest to me, whose sitting bones were lifted considerably higher than mine, had a tattoo stamped on her long neck. I wondered if she had a husband, if he drank and how much. The tattoo was a scorpion that appeared to be stinging her directly in the carotid artery. I felt briefly happy about my tattoo-free neck. I scanned the rest of the class for tattoos, for signs of alcohol-sodden marriages. My head heavy with blood and the backs of my knees creaking open, I made up terrible stories for each woman: pulled hair, punched faces, ruined children. I made up the sort of stories I imagined would be told in a support group, in a smoky room full of women who would nod and say, *Mmmm-hmmm, sister!* after each horrible revelation.

"Press *down* with the soles of the feet," Gisela said. "Your feet are grounded *firmly* on the earth and your sitting bones *reach* for the sky."

I pressed and reached, wondering what I would say if asked to spew a mess of condemning details about my husband, what I would say if I really tried to answer my mother's questions: *Honey, has he hit you?* Jay had never hit me, had never crashed our car or lost his job, had never called me names or pulled my hair. I shut my mouth tight and closed my eyes, as if to keep this secret locked in my head: Sometimes we had fun when he was drunk. If I could catch him between his third drink and his fourth we'd have sweet, sloppy sex. At times he cooked up a marijuana/alcohol buzz that made hysterical things spill out of his lovely mouth, and we'd laugh and maybe dance some, in our own living room. If we danced well to a song, Jay would play it on his show. If we couldn't get into the rhythm of it, if it didn't move us to gradually undress and lower the shades and dance in the way I dance only with Jay, naked and jiggling with my spirit swirling in my body, it was forever banned from *Revel Without a Pause*. I loved sending Jay off to work with a stack of CDs that had passed our naked-dancing test. It was as if he carried a part of me, a lock of my hair or a photo that showed the true color of my eyes.

Of course, a lot of it was awful, like the morning I woke up and saw bloody handprints mapping the wall of our bedroom. In the middle of the night my drunk husband had climbed the fence of a city pool and cut himself climbing back out. I was at home, sleeping, while he climbed, swam, climbed again, came home, and groped for the wall with his bloody hands. I woke up alone and saw the wall before I saw Jay on the floor in his wet clothes. *Who's screaming?* he said, his hands not hurting yet.

"You, Faith, open your *eyes*," Gisela said. "We keep our eyes *open* because the light gives us *energy*."

I jolted my eyes open, quickly ran through my list of things I could say about Jay's drinking: I hated the smell of beer? I hated the way beer seeped out of Jay's pores, that rotten, yeasty smell? I preferred my husband's eyes clear, rather than bloodshot? I hadn't yet found a cleaning agent that would take the smell of bong water out of carpet, and I didn't like spending my time thinking about cleaning products? I was tired of masturbating against an unconscious body? What the hell does a married woman have to do to get laid around here anyway?

Is he just knee-walking drunk every day? my mother had asked. No, Mother. *Honey, has he hit you?* No, Mother. But what he has done is enough. I want something better, for both of us.

"Yes," Gisela said, as if to answer me. "There, that's looking good, everyone. Now, relax into child's pose," Gisela said gently, and I slumped gratefully to the floor, remembering that no one had asked me to say anything, that all I had to do was stretch, extend, press and lift, open my eyes, and relax.

A Curveball Curves

I'd waited three long weeks without hearing from Jay, without even a hint that he might be ready to put down the bong and the bottle. Bottles. That should be *bottles*.

I didn't cry, and I didn't call anyone, except for a quick call to Darrah that consisted mostly of her saying, at the speed of an auctioneer, "Oh, listen, I'm on a deadline for this article about flesh-eating bacteria and I've got to pick up the baby in an hour."

My heart felt smaller and smaller; it felt like an apricot past its prime, shrinking and drying. I stumbled through my days, half frozen with hope. I ran mile after mile, my feet pounding out an angry chorus: *fuck* you *fuck* you *why why why*. I ran in the middle of the night, around the outdoor track, recklessly leaping hurdles on nights so dark I couldn't see where I would land.

I nearly burst into tears the morning I went up to the English department and saw that the remedial English T.A. had pinned a copy of Micah's latest vocabulary quiz to the bulletin board for the amusement of the other faculty. Circled in red was my poor baby's attempt to write a sentence demonstrating the meaning of the word *relatively:* "The two sisters were both dogs, making them relatively ugly." I tore it off the board and vowed to do better with Micah. I made him go running with me that night, and worked about ten sentences that included *relatively* into our conversation.

"You tryin' to tell me somethin'?" he said just into our fifth mile.

I drew closer and closer to all my boys, banging on their dorm room doors to demand a look at their sloppy papers and crumpled exams, circling the poolroom downstairs and threatening to unplug the video games. I drove by the apartments of my off-campus athletes and sat on their dirty couches and made them turn off their televisions and talk to me about English and history, about when to use the subjunctive tense in Spanish and about whether it would be McGwire or Griffey or Sosa who'd finally break the home run record. I was pulling for all of them. I was pulling for anybody with half a chance of having a good year.

I manically cheered my babies on as they beat Missouri, as they humiliated Rice, as they crushed A&M. I listened in on their conversations and interrupted whenever I heard a grammatical slip. I renewed my last year's campaign to stop the rampant misuse of *hopefully*. It was a word they abused on a daily basis, as in "Hopefully we'll win today." *No!* I'd yell from all the way down the hall. Sometimes I yelled a little too loudly, as if I were screaming at everything that had encroached on my marriage: every can of beer, every bottle of gin, every bag of weed, and the man who didn't seem willing to give up any of it. My marriage had dwindled down to this: my racing around and around the track at midnight, barely clearing hurdles in the dark.

One Tuesday evening I convinced Coach to impose a penalty of a hundred wind sprints on anyone who didn't attend the lecture I'd arranged on the physics of baseball. I had hired Heinz Fechtler, the lecturer, a few times in the past as a freelance tutor. This time I'd invited him because he was beautiful, in that superior blond Swiss way; because I had started to look ravenously at even the dimmest of my ballplayers; because the day before, when Cory Bell had approached me for his weekly attempt to match me up with Jesus Christ as my Lord and Savior, I had allowed him to take my hands and pray over me simply because it felt so damn good to have my hands enclosed in those of another human being. I didn't hear a word Cory said. I felt the warmth of his hands around mine and felt the rest of my body sort of lighting up and when Cory said, "Amen," I thought, *Oh shit, did I just accept Jesus Christ as my personal Lord and Savior or what?* Then Cory said, "Miss Evers, do you think you're ready to open your heart to the Lord yet?" and I said, "Not quite yet, honey," but I wanted to say, *Maybe if you held my hand just one more time . . .*

I was getting clobbered in the Game of Life.

I decided, in the hour between dinner and the physics lecture, to listen to Jay's show. I would listen for a sign. Either I would hear something that would give me the patience to wait a few more days, or I would hear something that would set me free. It started off badly; Jay had invited listeners to call in with their hangover remedies.

"How dare you!" I yelled at the radio.

Jay said what he always said at the start of the show: "The one cure we don't want to hear about here on Dr. Jay's call-in hour is hair of the dog. Remember, our motto is: Why have just a hair when you can have the whole dog?"

Something clicked off in my heart when Jay said that, though I had heard it many times before without the clicking.

"That's it," I said to Jay, as if he could hear me. "Just forget it."

I turned off the radio and went down to the video room, where I herded six or seven boys away from the foosball table. Then I walked up and down the halls, pounding on doors and repeating the threat of wind sprints.

"How'd the Spanish quiz go?" I asked Micah as I pried his fingers away from his TV's remote control.

"It's chill," he said.

Finally I had the entire team slouching around the study lounge in their combination of Jesus- and Nike-themed clothing while Heinz Fechtler, a forty-year-old physics grad student with a slight Swiss-German accent, tried to interest them in the science of their game. I stood at the back of the room, next to a tattered poster of Wade Boggs, and slowly unraveled my hair from its braid.

"The stitches on a baseball," Heinz Fechtler was saying, "make it travel through the air faster than if it were smooth. This reason is because the stitches make a turbulence that makes a boundary layer near the surface of the ball and this boundary layer reduces air friction. Here is an example for you: A smooth ball thrown with a velocity of one hundred miles per hour would, on reaching home plate, have a velocity of eighty-three miles per hour, but a ball with stitches thrown with a velocity of one hundred miles per hour would reach home plate with a velocity of ninety miles per hour."

"Leo Rhodes, stop slurping," I said. Leo glanced back at

me, then set his Big Gulp on the floor. Heinz nodded to me in appreciation, shifted his rimless glasses to a higher perch on his nose, and continued. It had been eight years since I'd made love with anyone but Jay. For the past five years I'd felt cheated on every time he raised a drink to his lips. I told myself our marriage was over. I told myself I was free to do whatever I wanted, never mind that what I wanted — Jay sober and in love with me — wasn't available. I would just have to want something else.

"Pitching trajectories we will talk about now. A fastball with an initial velocity of ninety-eight miles per hour will fall three feet on its way to the plate because of gravity, although backspin will lessen this drop slightly. The ball will cross the plate in four-tenths of a second at ninety miles per hour, having slowed about one mile per hour for each seven feet of travel."

I thought of the day, that day my junior year of college, when I was walking across campus full of intentions of coloring my hair red. Not Mother's light, beginning-of-a-sunset red, but a deep, end-of-a-sunset red. I watched the people who passed me, trying to find a girl with the shade of red I wanted. I imagined myself transformed; the redheaded me would be smarter, sexier, magically freed from a life sentence of listening to blonde jokes. From a distance I heard someone yelling my name. "Your hair!" this guy was yelling. "Your hair!"

Screw you and your whole dog, too. Screw every hair on your drunken head.

"A curveball curves," Heinz Fechtler was saying, "because its spin causes differences in air pressure on the sides of the ball. If the ball spins counterclockwise, for example, the air pressure is greater on the third-base side than on the first-base side, causing the ball to curve toward first base."

The boy yelling about my hair was Jay; I knew him from my history class. "Your hair!" he said again, when he was close enough to talk in a normal tone of voice. He was slightly out of breath. "The sun was on it — it was amazing!" I skipped my afternoon classes and we walked up the Drag and drank coffee together until we were so jittery that our hands sort of shook into each other, then we didn't stop touching. We had started to hurl ourselves, with great velocity, into the territory of love. I never colored my hair. Maybe I should have.

"Hey!" I said in the direction of a couple of whispering outfielders. "Just because you guys beat Stanford today does not mean you know everything there is to know about baseball. Shut up and listen to our guest."

"The bat and ball," Heinz Fechtler continued, "are in contact for about one thousandth of a second. During this time, a force of eight thousand pounds is required to change the direction of a ninety-mile-per-hour pitch to a one-hundred-and-ten-mile-per-hour hit that will travel four hundred feet. When this force is applied, the ball is compressed to about one half its diameter. Although most of the energy in the ball and bat is lost as heat, the baseball returns about thirty-five percent of the energy it receives during compression, and it is this energy that causes the ball to rebound from the bat."

Jay, Jay, Jay. His name suited the rhythm of my pulse, the bastard. I wished he had some clumsy name, one my body couldn't sing to so easily: Oscar, Norman, Nebuchadnezzar. I hated him for having something — booze — to keep him from going crazy with thoughts of me. I looked around the room, as if to find a corresponding something of my own. I scanned the walls of the study lounge, the posters of professional athletes: Jordan, Aikman, the beloved Nolan Ryan. Cory Bell leaned forward in his chair as if to show me the back of his T-shirt: "If You Can't Take the Heat, Stay Out of Hell." I looked and looked, from Leo's crumpled Big Gulp cup to the diagram, on the chalkboard at the front of the room, charting the erratic flight path of a knuckleball. My eyes settled on Heinz Fechtler, on his glossy blond hair, on the glasses skewed across his face, on his solemn mouth as he explained that a one-inch reduction in barometric pressure adds about six feet to the flight of a four-hundred-foot fly ball (so *that's* why Denver's annoyingly named Coors Field is a pitcher's graveyard), and I heard, in advance, the Mistress of Morals admonishing me for what I was about to do: "Bum sexuality. Get your sexuality back where it belongs, back into your committed relationship, I don't care how neglected you *feel,* and quit with the bumdom already."

When Heinz had finished his lecture, when my ballplayers had rushed out of the study lounge toward their TVs and video games and their enthusiastic little girlfriends, I asked Heinz if I could take him out for a beer.

"Certainly," he said.

"You did a great job," I told him.

"I don't know if I made it simple enough. It is so simple to me that I forget it is not so for everyone."

"It was perfect," I told him. "You gave us all a lot to think about."

In the dark, dampish bar filled mostly with grad students in dark clothes, a beautiful blond woman, almost white-blond, with extremely pale skin and a strong, wide face, glided past our table. I turned to watch her.

"We have thousands of her in Switzerland," Heinz said.

I resisted asking him how often his name prompted people to say, "Heinz like the ketchup?" I resisted telling him I was married, or revealing how many months it had been since I'd made love with a man who was conscious. I thought of Lucy, of her perfect eyebrows. I thought if I were a ball-player, I'd want to play center field; I'd want to be as far from home as possible.

Before I put my hand on his arm, before I made my first easy suggestion, I involuntarily thought of something about Jay that I liked very much: despite his brunette hair, he never told blonde jokes. If someone else told one in front of him, he'd say, "Well, my wife's blond and that doesn't sound anything like her." I took a deep breath, knowing that soon a little more of Jay would be gone. And why not? He had gradually washed himself from me, drop by alcoholic drop. Why shouldn't I finish the job? I would have to get on with things some time. Why not start right away?

"I am so old for you," Heinz Fechtler said when we were both naked in his dark room, his room filled with books in a language I didn't know. After all those nights of rubbing my naked self against Jay's unconscious lips, it was amazing to be actively kissed. It's amazing that people with someone to kiss ever get anything else done.

"I'm not so young," I said. I felt a hundred years old.

"Yes, but you have a young body," he said, his face rough, alive, against mine. They were the nicest words I'd heard in a while, and I planned to hold on to them through the long and lovely night to come.

Rope

During the hours I spent in his bed, Heinz was completely and deliciously fun. Of course, my standards had been systematically lowered (*A man's in bed with me and he's awake and he doesn't smell like a microbrewery? Yeee-haw!*) so I wasn't exactly picky. But I did enjoy making Heinz so delirious that he lapsed into his mother tongue; I enjoyed dreaming up my own translation of his thick and densely textured language. But the next morning I stood in the shower and cried for half an hour under the hottest water I could stand. Giving up Jay, I felt a heightened version of the sadness I felt whenever one of my athletes dropped out or was expelled: something I'd worked very hard on had gone unfinished.

I flipped open Jay's spiral notebook and let my wet hair drip all over it. Insanely hoping for wisdom, I found this offering from a listener in Bastrop: "Great show, man. And I've got a great cure for you. Either masturbate or have sex at least twice before you go to sleep. Is that okay? Can I say masturbate on the radio?"

Just as I slammed the notebook shut, Coach's secretary phoned me to come into his office.

"Micah failed his Spanish quiz with a sixty-four," Coach said when I was barely through the door. "My blood pressure is through the roof, Faith." He leaned against the edge of his gray metal desk. He wore burnt orange polyester shorts which outlined his genitals in a painful (for me) and depressing way. His face was hard and male and sun-dried except for a glaze of saliva on his lips that I wished he'd do something about. Coach suffered from what one of my staffers had called "saliva issues." I finally rested my eyes on the shelf of trophies behind his desk, trophies the color of elderly, fake blondes.

"I worked with him as much as I possibly could have," I said. "I knocked on his door and made him turn off the TV and I quizzed him even when he didn't want me to. He had it down. He must have choked. Of course it would help if he gave a damn."

"Look, Faith, I pulled some strings; no, make that rope — I pulled some big-ass rope — and the prof's going to give him a makeup quiz first thing Monday morning and take the average of the two grades. So the failing grade doesn't go into his weekly average yet, which means he can still pitch Friday in Houston. But I want you to go with us. Please, Faith. You can work with him on the bus, you can sit in the goddamn bullpen if you have to, but I want him ready for that makeup test. His eligibility to start against Miami depends on this grade. You know I'll have hell to pay if I have to pull Micah, and so will you."

"Hell to pay? After I've singlehandedly dragged Cory Bell's GPA up to a stunning two point nine?" But I knew what he was talking about. Micah had thrown a no-hitter against Miami the year before, and the press would surely take notice of this game more than any we'd played so far.

"Bell isn't the one the alums are hot to see, Faith. Bell isn't the one who turned down a major league contract 'cause his mama wants him to get a degree first. The stolen-base thing is nice, don't get me wrong, but it doesn't get the same kind of press as Micah throwing a no-no. You know how it is, Faith. Which, by the way, I'd like to move Tommy Cox out of your program and into Anne's. We pay you to focus on the stars, not kids like Tommy."

"I know, but I'd like to see Tommy graduate. You know damn well he's not going to make it even to the minors, so he needs a degree. And he's very close."

"Get Micah through this and you can keep Tommy."

"What time does the bus leave?" I said, wondering if my visit to Houston would include a viewing of Mother's giant tomato.

"Eight A.M., sharp. *Buena suerte*," he said with a wink. I stared at him, unable to believe that a man in polyester shorts was wishing *me* luck.

"*Gracias*," I said, and turned to leave.

Definitely a Genius

While I packed for the Houston trip, I tried listening to a Miles Davis CD. I tried to ignore the fact that Jay's show was on right that minute. I tried to remember how much I love Miles Davis. He blew "Surrey with the Fringe on Top," a song that has never once brought to my mind either surreys or fringe. Near the end of the song, I cut him off rudely and flipped the switch on my box from CD to radio. Jay was playing, as he had been rather frequently, Lyle Lovett's version of "Stand By Your Man."

Someone knocked on my door halfway through the song. I thought it would be one of my ballplayers, someone with an essay to write or a Spanish verb to conjugate or a novel for which no video existed. But instead it was Darrah, without the baby.

"Hey," I said, giving her a hug. "How'd you escape?"

"Danny's home with her," she said. "I told him I had to get out for a few minutes."

"Sing it, Lyle!" Jay broke in over the song's chorus.

"Faith!" Darrah said, flopping onto my bed. "Why are you listening to that?"

"That," I said, "is my husband."

"That," she said, "is the guy who was blazing drunk last time I was at your house. He's standing by the turntable on his drunken wobbly feet playing some album way too loud and yelling, 'I like a needle in my music, Buddy! Yeah, gimme those pops and hisses!' I mean, it's a wonder the guy isn't a heroin addict or something. But of course, Jay wouldn't have time for heroin — he's too busy drinking." Darrah's face was still plump from her pregnancy. Her expressions took longer to rise to the surface; they weren't as exposed as they had been on her sharp, angular, prepregnancy face, but still, her disgust was plain.

"Since when is it a crime to listen to the radio?" I said.

"Faith, I've known you ten years. I've known Jay almost that long. The guy's a hard-core addict. I know you've always had this fantasy that he'd get more addicted to your love than he is to booze and weed, but the man would sell his grandmother's soul for a glass of gin and you know it."

"I know." Now I wished Cory would knock on the door, or that Micah would come slouching in with lists of Spanish vocabulary.

"It's not that you're not worthy of being loved more than a bunch of booze and drugs, it's just . . . the guy's a sicko."

"I hear you, Darrah. But let's talk about something else, okay?"

"Hey," she said, "guess what the baby's doing now."

"What?"

"She can get her toes all the way up to her mouth and suck on them. We think she's a genius."

"Definitely a genius. How's the peach tree?"

"I think it's alive," she said.

"I fucked someone last night," I said.

"No kidding," Darrah said. "I'm amazed."

"I know. It was a grad student. A one-time thing, probably."

"Was it fun? Was he sensitive?" *Sensitive* was our code for *Did he give you oral sex and a sufficient amount of it?*

"Yeah, it was great. He was extremely sensitive." Darrah laughed. "But I felt like shit this morning."

"Faith, the guy's fucked you six ways to Sunday. He may not have cheated on you, but he's screwed you over on multiple occasions and if he did have a mistress, I bet she wouldn't have caused nearly as much trouble as his drinking has."

"I know. It's over between us. I know that. I just have to get used to it, you know? It's just going to take a while."

"Well, maybe you'd get used to it faster if you found another radio station to listen to."

"I know. You're right."

The "Stand By Your Man" phase of the show had ended and now Jay was playing a Neville Brothers song, a song we had grown to love on our honeymoon, a song that had passed our naked-dancing test many times. I stared very hard at Darrah's short, reddish hair and tried not to cry. I don't even like the Neville Brothers that much. But when a girl has danced naked to a song with the man she loves, that song has a power over her forever.

"Oh, Jesus, now I suppose we'll have to listen to him talk," Darrah said as the song ended. "This is KXAL," Darrah said in imitation of Jay, "spinning the background music for your drunken binge —"

"Shut up," I said.

When Jay started to talk, I half expected him to say,

"Don't cry, Buddy. Come on, Buddy, it's okay." But instead he said something far better, something so good that even Darrah quieted down to listen: "I'm Jason Evers and this is *Revel Without a Pause* and day two of the High on Wife Marathon, starring yours truly as the drunk guy trying to get clean. High on life? Sure thing, my gentle and nongentle listeners, but I'll be high on my wife, my beautiful Faith Anne Abbott Evers with the long blond hair and the cutlery-sharp mind and the smile that could sell stereos to the deaf, the day she comes back to me. Should she? Would she? I can only hope. I have been sober for twenty-seven hours now and boy does it hurt, but it would hurt a heck of a lot more without your calls of support. Thank you all for your kind words, for your descriptions of your own personal higher powers, for your many home remedies: ginger tea, milk this-tle, a good headstand once an hour. Thank you to the lis-tener who sent the peach cobbler; it was top-notch, and I'm in just the position to appreciate a good sugar high, if you know what I mean. But I'd especially like to thank those of you who have pledged support to our High on Wife hotline. Your donations go directly to help the families of people killed and maimed by drunk drivers, by arrogant, selfish drunks like yours truly. I've never killed or maimed anyone, but I could have. I sure could have. There but for the grace of You Know Who and so on and so forth. So call that hotline, call 474-HIGH, and give a little to help some people whose lives have been pretty heavily stomped on. I'll be here for twenty-six days straight, yes, right here with Gracie the cat. The houseplants are doomed. My fridge will become a sci-ence project. But I'll be right here on the marathon to sobri-ety for twenty-six wrenching days, broadcasting all day and all night except for those sacred hours of six-thirty A.M. to ten-thirty A.M. when the Mistress of Morals arrives to whip us all into shape. I'll be taking your calls, I'll be hosting nationally known experts on alcoholism, I'll be begging for your money, and, as always, I'll be spinning the tunes you crave. We had a request for this one and here it is, local treasure Nicole Austin with her *muy* soulful rendition of 'Miss Celie's Blues.'"

By the time the song started, I had the volume turned all the way up; its sound was muffled, distorted, beautiful. I wished I could rewind it, wished I could hear one more time my husband saying "starring yours truly as the drunk guy trying to get clean."

Darrah and I stared at each other. She reached to turn down the volume.

"Do you think hell's freezing over as well?" she said.

"God, Darrah!" I said. "It's like you almost *want* my life to suck. I mean, you've got your lawyer husband who reads feminist literature and quotes Shakespeare while you fuck and your beautiful house and your genius baby and you just can't give me an inch! You make me feel like such a loser!"

"I'm sorry," she said. "Of course you're not a loser. You're my favorite woman in the whole wide world." She moved closer to me on the bed, close enough so she could put her hand on my knee and pick at the hole in my jeans. She pulled out thread after thread from either side of the hole, smoothing them toward each other over the tight bare skin of my knee. "I know it sounds good," she said. "But I just hate to see you get your hopes up again. It could just be a promotion for the radio station, Faith. It could be bullshit.

Or he could mean it but tomorrow when he wants a drink the whole thing'll be out the window. Just don't rush over there tonight. Give it a few days. Please, just wait and see."

"I wish he had told me he was planning this," I said, realizing that the marathon must have already been in the works the night I was with Heinz. "I never would have . . ."

"Don't beat yourself up about it," Darrah said. "Please, Faith. Any other woman would have given up on Jay long ago. You just have this toughness, you know, where you think you can make these bimbo athletes into Rhodes scholars and you think you can make your drunk husband sober and when it doesn't work out you just grab on harder, like a pit bull or something."

"Could you please compare me to something more attractive than a pit bull?"

"Don't go over there."

"I have to go to Houston for a couple of days anyway," I said.

"With the team?"

"Yeah. See, the Longhorns are planning to *hook* the Cougars. Or they might *spear* the Cougars. They might even *trample* the Cougars. Just depends on what fabulous imagery the cheerleaders have come up with this week."

"So at least wait until after Houston. Please," she said. "Promise me."

I thought about it for a minute, about how Darrah could be right. But I decided that even if the whole thing was a big lie, some sort of promotion for the station that had nothing to do with our real lives, I would still enjoy it for a few days. I would go to Houston and tell my mother what a wonderful thing Jay was doing; I would make Micah so fluent as to shock his perhaps-lesbian professor; I would waltz around the University of Houston campus like I had everything to look forward to, like all my wishes had come true.

"Okay," I told Darrah. "I promise."

U-Can-Dig-It

I decided to visit my parents during the first game of the Houston doubleheader, the game Micah was pitching. I figured if he went the distance, which he usually did, I'd have a couple of hours free and clear. If he got knocked out in the early innings, he'd be too cranky to work on his Spanish anyway.

I called my mother from a pay phone and asked if she could come pick me up, if she might want to get some lunch and hear my good news.

"Sugar," she said, "you've just got to see my tomato! I'm absolutely in love with it."

"Lucky you," I said. I thought how nice it must be to be absolutely in love with something that can't talk back, something that can't smash your heart. Had I not said the words *good news* loudly enough?

"I *am* lucky," she sang. "And I'm on my way."

In the car I watched her profile, tight except for a looseness just under her chin. Her red-blond hair was screwed into a bun; dirt and grass stains marked her shorts and T-shirt.

"I'm a mess," she said. "I've been digging all morning

with my brand-new shovel. It's called a U-Can-Dig-It. It has these spiky things on the end and it's just heaven. As far as digging goes, I mean."

"Mother, I know you love to dig, so don't pretend."

"I do. I turned my whole compost pile over this morning. I've got beautiful compost this year, honey. I've been running all over town getting old coffee grounds from the coffee shops. That's my new secret."

Many of my mother's sentences begin with *this year*. She's always starting over, forgetting about the cutworms, the drought, the aphids of last year. Her life is full of new chances.

"I wish I'd known, Mother. I would have brought you some from the cafeteria."

"Oh, honey, I wish you had! They're just like gold."

I wished she would ask me what my good news was. I guess I could have just blurted out, "Guess what! Jay's getting sober!" But I wanted her to ask me. I wanted her to shut up about her gardening secrets for two seconds and just say, "How *are* you, Sugar?" But it was things like her U-Can-Dig-It shovel and her truckloads of coffee grounds that kept Mother from seeing my busted-up heart and the chance I had of putting it back together. I envied her her easy loves.

"Is Daddy home?" I said.

"Oh no, honey, he's at the hospital. You know Friday's a big day over there. He couldn't get away, but he told me to hug your neck. Are you sure you can't stay the night?"

"I wish I could, but I need to stay at the hotel with the team. My star pitcher is having an academic crisis." I knew that Daddy had not told Mother to hug my neck. My father does not say things about wanting to hug someone's neck or about being absolutely in love with a tomato. He performs his surgeries, and he drinks, quietly.

"See the top of it?" Mother said as we pulled into the driveway.

Looming above the high stone wall was something that could only be described as a tomato tree. It reminded me of a very thin woman, her arms flung up in happiness.

"Mother, that's the biggest plant I've ever seen," I said.

"I'm so glad you think so, honey! Come on," she said, practically dragging me through the gate. Then we stopped, and quieted, as if we were approaching a holy place. The tomato plant was about fourteen feet high, supported by a huge cylinder of concrete reinforcing wire. Near the middle of the plant was the tomato Mother had chosen to coax to the title of World's Largest; she'd pinched off the other flowers so the plant could channel all of its energy into the single fruit.

Mother dragged a stepladder from the back porch and stood on it to draw back the leaves shading the giant green globe.

"Look at my baby," she said, in a soothing, quiet voice, the kind of voice one might use to speak to a human infant. "Isn't it the biggest damn thing? The six o'clock news came out and did a piece on it a week ago, and now I've got every tomato freak in Harris County flocking over here to see it, and all kinds of invitations to talk to gardening clubs and you wouldn't believe."

The tomato was still a pale green, but it was the size of an infant's head.

"It's incredible," I said. I thought of what my father always says when someone wants to show him a new baby, expecting him to comment on its cuteness. He summons his most enthusiastic voice and says, "My God! That *is* a baby!"

"It needs to weigh thirteen pounds and seven ounces to beat the record," Mother said. "If nothing goes wrong, I should make it. But so many things can go wrong, of course." Those things were the ones I'd heard about all my life: cutworms, nematodes, early blight, vermicullum wilt. But I thought of the thing that had been wrong in my life, desperately wrong, the thing that was perhaps being fixed right that minute, and I wanted to knock Mother off her ladder for not even caring; I wanted to grab that giant tomato and smash it against the house.

"Mother," I said. "Do you give a damn about anything besides your garden?"

I closed my eyes and thought of something from Jay's list of hangover cures: "Give up drinking and smoke herb instead."

"What do you mean, honey?"

"Aren't you even going to ask me how I am? If I'm still separated from Jay?"

"Of course, honey," she said. Still on the ladder, she loomed over me like some tomato-eating Amazon. "How are you?" she said.

But it was too late, and I was too angry. I was a child again, standing in the darkened window of my bedroom, watching Mother weed her garden by the light of the moon and wishing she'd come up and read me a story, kiss my forehead, tell me I was a dear and sweet girl.

"Fine," I said. "I'm fine."

"Well, good, honey. I knew you were. You *look* wonderful."

I turned away from the tomato, but the rest of the yard was also filled with living, growing things, things that were flourishing under my mother's loving attentions. I walked over to a bed of mint and knelt down to touch it; I breathed in its cool, clean scent, and it cleared some of the junk from my head. Excess love for Jay flew around my heart like shrapnel. I think if I could have shaken that feeling, that shrapnel-in-the-heart feeling, I could have let Mother have her giant tomato, and I could have been happy for her. We could have been two women who were deeply in love, who had both found things worth working on.

"Do you want to see my okra?" Mother said.

"No!" I said, standing up. "Jesus, Mother! You have no idea what's going on with me and you don't even care! Just stay away from me!"

"Well, of course I care!" she called after me as I ran into the house to phone for a cab. Mother didn't follow me.

Next to the phone was Daddy's knitting; I touched the rough yarn as I told the taxi operator our address. Daddy knit between surgeries to keep his hands nimble; he knew only one stitch, learned from his med school roommate and called, wonderfully, Mistake Stitch Ribbing. He'd knit it until he'd used up a ball of yarn, then he'd set aside the piece and start another one. It bothered me that he didn't knit anything in particular. I used to say, "Why don't you do a blanket or a scarf or something?"

"I don't want to," he'd say simply, then he'd go on knitting, more and more recklessly as the night wore on and his vodka intake increased. He didn't worry about the mistakes; he just went on. This was the difference between my parents: If Mother had been a knitter, she would have made fabulous, intricate creations. She would have set some sort of bizarre world record for knitting. This was the similarity between my parents: They had always had projects that absorbed them completely, projects that weren't me.

I waited for the taxi on the front steps and Mother didn't come out to talk to me. While I sat there, I stroked a branch of the huge rosemary bush that crowded the front steps and wondered if Jay had been taking care of our own potted rosemary plant. Mother had taught us how to pet the rosemary, to release the oils that keep it healthy. Jay liked to yank on it when he was high, to stand over it and breathe the clean, forest-scented air. *Don't yank, Jay, just pet it,* I'd say.

After a minute an ancient white Cadillac pulled up in front of the house and a group of old ladies shoved out of it and bustled up the walk.

"Is this where we see the tomato?" said one of the women. She wore a sun hat ringed in tiny plastic cacti and a T-shirt that said, "Compost Happens."

"I don't know," I said. "I guess you could ring the doorbell and ask."

When Mother answered the door she said, "Oh, you must be here about the tomato!" and before the door even closed behind them I could hear her launching into her speech about her gardening methods: building the soil, planting with the moon's phases, using seaweed and fish emulsion as fertilizer. So what. I ran toward the cab when it pulled up at the end of the brick walk, anxious to get back to my ballplayers. At least they were occasionally interested in what I had to say, and I loved them for it.

Goin' Down the Road Feelin' Bad

When our bus finally arrived back on campus in Austin, my ballplayers galloped toward the dorm, still pumped up about their series sweep of Houston. I leaned against the dirty bus, not wanting to go up to my empty room.

"Miss Evers, can I carry your bag for you?" Cory said. When I ignored the shaved number on top of Cory's skull, his hair, the length of AstroTurf, made him look like a little boy who had just been taken to get his summer haircut.

"*May* I carry your bag," I said.

"Miss Evers, I'd never let you carry my bag. *I* want to carry *your* bag, is what I'm sayin'."

"Sure, honey," I said. "Why don't you take it up for me. I'm going to go for a drive."

I walked across the hot parking lot to my Chevelle and drove to the radio station, then sat outside in the car listening to my husband talk. I don't know why I didn't go in, why being a few hundred yards away from Jay made me miss him a little less, why it almost chased away the fatigue from the Houston trip. I sat there and thought of things I knew about his body. I thought of the bump on his chest where his breastbone had been broken and hadn't healed right. I thought of the tiny scar above his right eyebrow, where he'd fallen in a parking lot, drunk probably, and hit the edge of a car's bumper. His torso, absolutely hairless except for a very fine fur that I had to rest my head on his chest to see. I thought of his lips, which were often chapped, and which felt wonderful pressed against any old part of me. I've since learned that alcoholics often have chapped lips, or small tears at the corners of their lips, due to a lack of nutrients. I've learned a thousand other things as well, and if I'd known what they were to be, if I'd known what was to come, sitting in my car that night, I would have started up the motor and peeled out of the parking lot and driven as far as my Chevelle would carry me. But instead I sat there, Jerry Garcia singing "How Sweet It Is" on the radio, my forehead on the steering wheel, determined to keep every inch of Jay's being present in my mind, determined to keep something of him whether this marathon was a dream come true or just another potential heartbreak or both. I had a brief scare when I couldn't remember his hands. Were the nails ridged or smooth, narrow or wide? I could picture the knuckles, and the hands themselves, but the nails were vague and I scrambled for a mental picture of them, ransacking my mind the way you'd tear up a room looking for car keys. Finally I remembered, I found a memory of his hand when he'd cut it during one of his exuberant bursts of cooking: The nails were wide, but not flat like some men's; they had a nice arc to them.

"Stop it," I said out loud. But it was time to trade one anguish for another anyway, because the song had ended and Jay started talking.

"That was the Jerry Garcia Band and my own personal

tribute to an old pal from college, a kid we called Frantic José. He came into freshman year plagued by the conflicting roars of a Cubano-Catholic morality and the Carlos Castaneda–Jerry Garcia jam going on in his rather hefty intellect. This smart kid from Queens entered Texas in love with ZZTop and little crew girls named Missy, and left on acid. In between he found himself a big earth mother Deadhead of a girlfriend; I mean I wouldn't have crossed the woman for anything, I was afraid she'd *deck* me. This earth mother and I ended up on the South Mall one night, blitzed on mushrooms, waiting for Frantic José to get his van going and get us out to Manor Downs for a dose of the good ol' Grateful Dead. I had it all going on, I'm willing to admit: the tie-dyed T-shirt complete with Dead lyrics: 'Once in a while you get shown the light/In the strangest of places if you look at it right.' I had the sandals made from old tires, the little leather pouch around my neck with my goodies in it. I had the old ripped up army shorts with a Steal Your Face patch sewn on the back pocket. I smelled like patchouli and looked like a rich homeless kid. And I had my little whirling-dervish dance moves, which I might have been willing to practice out on the mall if the trees hadn't started skidding, and skidding at high speed. I sat down in the grass, to make sure I stayed still while the trees zipped by me. The earth mother drifted away and I became extremely involved with a blade of grass near the toe of one of my used-tire sandals and I never did make it out to Manor Downs that night. At one point the trees were moving so fast I thought they were taking all the air with them, that there wasn't enough oxygen left behind for me to breathe. I considered standing up, asserting myself, and demanding my share of Oh-two, but instead I stretched out on the grass and opened my lips wide, hoping enough air would fall into my mouth to keep me going. A girl walked by, handed me a peach, and kept walking. A peach, my gentle and nongentle listeners. This peach was to see me through the difficult night ahead; it would become my comfort and my friend. I smelled it until it didn't have a smell anymore. Later, when I told my brother, the doctor, about sniffing the smell clean out of the peach, he told me there was an explanation for why I had *ceased to smell the peach,* as he put it. I begged him not to burst my little psychedelic bubble. I declined, hands clamped over my ears, to hear his logical explanation. I had held that peach and loved it through the long hours of the night, and it had been a glowing, gorgeous, perfumed miracle. The next morning, when I slowly reeled my brain back into my skull, I saw that my peach was looking a little *peaked,* shall we say, slightly bruised and nicked and generally overloved. It was no longer edible, or even viewable. The girl who had given me that peach was my friend Faith, who later became my wife, my glowing, gorgeous, miracle of a wife. And now I've sniffed all the lovely scent out of her, if you'll excuse the disgusting imagery; I've left her bruised and nicked. And here we are at the start of another long night, and peaches aren't yet in season, and my Faith is nowhere to be seen. I'd like to think Frantic José and his earth mother of a girlfriend are still happy, still in love, still spinning and bopping to some groovy Grateful Dead tune, and although I know it ain't so I hope you'll allow me my boyish fantasy for at least one more song. Here's the good ol' GD with 'Goin' Down the Road Feelin' Bad,' dedicated to you, of course."

It was amazing to me how Jay could take a story about

Frantic José, whom I'd always despised, and coat it in love and nostalgia until even I was longing to be back in college, waltzing across the mall with a bag of peaches, stopping to hand one to a boy sitting in the grass who would later become my husband. But no wonder I looked back, no wonder even a sleazy acid dealer like Frantic José was welcome in my memories. The present was excruciating, each moment shrieking against my heart like fingernails on a chalkboard as I tried to trust, once again, that Jay would stop drinking. The future was terrifying; if Jay didn't stop this time, I would have to shake him from my heart. Only the distant past was full, and warm, and lovely in retrospect. So I stared back at it like it was a gorgeous painting, or a gleaming sculpture; then I started my car and drove away.

It's a Hard Road, Faith

Each Monday morning I walked around campus and talked to as many professors as I could about my ballplayers. I tried to find out which had bad attitudes, which were making an effort, which needed to have some Texas-size strings pulled on their behalf.

I tried to accept the veiled insults, the little jabs about my profession, with grace and poise.

My third stop of the morning on the post-Houston Monday was Dr. Stanley, the physiology professor, his class one of my big success stories: a 96 percent passing rate for my baseball players, 92 percent for my football players during my four years as head tutor. The credit was due more to Dr. Stanley than to me; he taught my boys all about their bodies, about the blood and bones and muscle and how they coordinated to hit home runs and catch long passes. He had a love of the body that allowed him to appreciate my athletes for what they were, such fine examples of human physiology. And, on the Monday morning when I was paralyzed with fear that Jay's marathon was just a big promotion for KXAL, when I was terrified that I'd go to the station and find him sitting there with a stupid Busch beer, yammering into the microphone about sobriety, Dr. Stanley said he had good news for me. I was desperate for it.

"Faith!" he said. "How's tricks, dear?"

"Depends on what the good news is."

"A certain second baseman has stunned us all by earning a ninety-two on his first exam."

"You're kidding."

He held out Cory Bell's exam paper for me to see. It was lovely and pristine, almost completely free of red marks. I wanted to frame it.

"Think he came by this good fortune honestly?" Dr. Stanley said.

"Cory's not a cheater," I said. "He's a Holy Roller. He's always after me to accept Jesus Christ into my heart as my personal Lord and Savior."

"Ah," Dr. Stanley said, removing his glasses. His nose was pinched with red marks on both sides, where they had rested. Without the glasses he looked exposed, almost sunburned. "No offense, Faith."

"None taken." I stared for a moment at the poster of a human skeleton behind his desk. I imagined the skeleton dressed like Dr. Stanley: Birkenstocks, rumpled shirt, coffee-stained pants. "Could I ask you a question?" I said.

"Certainly."

"Could you tell me something about the physiology of alcoholism?"

"Writing a paper?"

"Trying to stay married."

"Ah. I was just reading something the other day," he said,

glasses back on, "by a doctor who's interested in treating alcoholics through nutrition. She wrote specifically about the alcoholic's reduced ability to absorb the nutrients in food. Their brains tend to get a bit out of whack, you might say, either through poor eating habits or because alcohol itself is a sugar, then the neurotransmitters responsible for emotions and stability don't operate smoothly, and a person becomes reliant on alcohol for a sense of well-being. It doesn't last, of course, the well-being. They typically experience wild swings in insulin and adrenaline, and they're constantly trying to correct their withdrawal symptoms with coffee, cigarettes, what have you. I'll try to find the article for you, but . . ." He threw up his hands as if to surrender to his desk and its wild landscape of books and papers and medical journals. "It's a hard road, Faith."

"I know, but I think I can do it."

"Well, every marriage has problems. Perhaps it's a matter of whether you want to work on the problems you have or trade them in for a new set."

"Thanks for the good news about Cory."

"You're doing a fine job, Faith. I think these boys might actually be in danger of learning something."

"I wish I could join them," I told him. "I'm feeling a little stupid these days."

"Nonsense!" he called after me as I walked out of his office. "Nonsense!"

Halfway between Dr. Stanley's office and the English department, when I was replaying what he'd said with the word *Jay* substituted for *alcoholic,* Micah Levin ran up behind me and clapped his giant hand down on my shoulder. I almost didn't recognize him with that big smile on his face; he could throw a no-hitter and still not crack a smile.

"You passed?"

"Eighty-eight."

"Micah, that's great! I'm so relieved."

"Let's go party, Miss Evers! Drink some beers, smoke some shit."

"Don't you even think about it," I said.

"Just messin' with you. I am gonna get drunk, though. I'm gonna start in about five minutes."

"You have History of the Earth in five minutes, Micah Levin, and you cannot afford to miss that class."

"Yeah, yeah."

"It's only noon, Mic. You can celebrate later. Come on, I'll go with you. I need to see what's going on in there anyway."

"Shit," he said. "I should've run the other way when I seen you. Don't know what I was thinking."

"When you *saw* me," I said. "I don't know why I worry about teaching you Spanish when your English is such a mess. Let's go," I said, and we did.

Dr. Cone's lecture that day was, in direct contrast to the course's title, about the future of the earth. I remember he said that in about thirty million years the movement of the earth's crust along the San Andreas Fault will have tugged Los Angeles to a position alongside San Francisco. In ten million years, he said, the Rocky Mountains and the Alps will have succumbed to erosion, while the Himalayas, thanks to continued wedging of the Indian Peninsula beneath them, will still stand tall. I was busy wondering whether Jay and I would be like the Rockies or the Himalayas, whether life would erode us or lift us up, when I saw that Micah had fallen asleep. His head rested heavily on his nonpitching hand; his dreadlocks draped his skull like tiny, wet cigars. I slipped his pen from his other hand, his notebook from his lap, and started taking notes.

Dear Jesus

On the sixth night of Jay's sobriety marathon, I sat in the parking lot of the radio station for an hour without going in. I sat there through a reading of excerpts from the works of famous alcoholic writers, thinking I'd go in as soon as the Faulkner section was over, then the Raymond Carver portion, then I almost had my nerve up toward the end of the Tennessee Williams section, before I finally gave up and drove back to the dorms. My ballplayers weren't in bed, even though it was past their curfew. I found them slumped in the study lounge, Big Gulps and pizza boxes all over the place, no one saying anything.

"Why aren't you future millionaires getting your beauty rest?" I said.

They stared at me with big, sad faces; somehow, they reminded me of cows. Finally Cory Bell, whose T-shirt that night read "Jesus Is Coming! Everyone Look Busy!" said, "Micah got caught with drugs, Miss Evers. He's off the team."

"He got caught by Coach?" This seemed impossible to me; Micah could have had a needle the size of a javelin hanging out of his arm and Coach would have managed to look the other way.

"By the campus cops. He ran his car into a pole in the east lot and passed out and they found some coke on him. Coach went ballistic on all of us, screaming and stuff."

"Yeah, the spit was flyin'," said Mike "Mr. Fuck This *Book* Shit" Winston. Mike had trimmed his stringy goatee into a squarish shape; when he talked, it gave his face the stiff-jawed look of a ventriloquist's dummy.

"I can't believe it," I said, sinking down into a chair. "I can't believe Micah's gone."

"Miss Evers," Cory said, "what if people, you know, the newspapers and stuff, think we're all doin' drugs over here?"

"Don't worry about what other people think, honey."

"But Miss Evers, the Bible says a good name is more desirable than great riches. And now our team's good name is sorta, you know . . ." He searched for a nonobscene word, finally settling on "messed-up."

"Screwed," Mike Winston said.

"My dear," I said to Cory, "a good lefty is more desirable than great riches, too." Without Micah, our starting rotation would consist entirely of right-handers, not a good thing at all.

Mike said, "Coach came and got all his shit and threw it out the dorm window. Fucked up his stereo and a bunch of other shit. Me and Leo stashed all his crap in our cars."

"Leo and I," I said.

"Whatever," Mike said.

"And he was supposed to start tomorrow," I said. "He passed his quiz today."

"Our season's fucked," Jamie Huston said.

"Let's have a prayer, you guys," Cory said.

"Fuck that," Mike said. "Fuckin' Jesus freak! Fuckin' faggot!"

"Michael, cut it out right now," I said. "Cory's got his way of dealing with things and you've got yours, so let's just try to respect each other, okay?"

"I'm not sayin' a prayer, man," Mike said. "You're not spewing your Jesus crap on me, Bell. Maybe Miss Evers'll put up with it, but she's fuckin' gettin' *paid,* man."

"Not enough," I said.

"We got something called freedom of religion in this country," Cory said. "In case you ain't heard. It's right there in the Declaration of Independence."

"*Haven't* heard," I said. "Bill of Rights," I said.

Cory dropped from the chair to his knees, folded his hands, closed his eyes, and said, "Dear Jesus, my God and Father, I ask You to be with Micah in his time of trouble."

"Shut up, Bell!" Mike said.

"Please give him strength, and wisdom, and help him to know that there's a power out there that's a lot greater than he is."

"I *said* shut up!" Mike stood and gave Cory's shoulder a push. Cory squeezed his closed eyes, and said, "Lord, maybe this is like a chance for Micah to turn his life around, to open up his heart for You to come in as his Lord and Savior."

"Michael," I said, because I could see that something had snapped in our big shortstop, in tall, strong Mike Winston who also played UT football, who wasn't used to not getting his way. Other guys were starting to say, "Chill, Winston," and I stood to put a hand on his arm as he loomed over the kneeling Cory, Mike's face red and his goatee devilish and his neck tense against the slimy gold chain that surrounded it, and I touched him just in time to feel the muscles of his arm move in concert with his leg as he reared back and kicked Cory swiftly in the ribs. The cracking sound might as well have been a bullhorn blaring, "End of season!"

"I said shut up!" Mike said. He turned and shoved his way out the door.

"Amen," Cory gasped from the floor.

"Cory, you stay quiet and hold still," I said. "I'm going to go page Coach and we'll get you some help, okay?" I knelt down and gave his crew cut a rub over the shiny skin of the bared number seven. "Everything's going to be fine, honey."

Even as I said it, I knew that everything was probably not going to be fine. I knew that Cory had lost his shot at the college stolen-base record, that the team had lost its shot at the college world series, that my job might be in danger without Cory and Micah and Mike to look after and with football season months away. But Jay supposedly was trying to stop drinking, and I was full of hopes that it was true, that he'd be mine again, and as long as that was possible I really didn't care about anything else.

I Hope That Answers Your Question

Darrah called nine days into Jay's sobriety marathon and said, "Have you seen him yet?"

"No, not yet," I said. I was bent over, lacing up my running shoes, the phone crammed between my shoulder and ear.

"Afraid to find out it's bullshit?"

"You need to ask?"

"Come see the baby this week. She's doing cool stuff."

"Such as?"

"Such as now she can make this sort of protracted vowel sound."

"She's brilliant," I said. "She must take after you."

While I ran around the hot noonday track, dodging sprinters and trainers with orange bullhorns, I thought about what Darrah had said, about why I hadn't gone to see Jay, and I waited for the real answer to surface in my mind. It had been fun, that week, to hear on the six o'clock news about a local deejay and his marathon for sobriety, to hear that other people wanting to get clean had started to gather in the lobby of the station, and that an AA group had started meeting in the lobby as well, even though Jay wasn't doing his sobriety through AA, even though he was doing it in his own weird Jay-type way. It had been fun for me to turn on the radio and hear Jay answer a caller's question about what the heck was wrong with AA and did he think he was too good for a program that had brought millions of people to sobriety? It was fun to hear him say, "Well, I'm getting sober to save my marriage, my marriage to a woman named Faith. Now, Faith has a lot of little pet peeves: She doesn't like the toilet seat left up; she hates it when the mail is all junk; she freaks when people use the word *hopefully* to modify a sentence, as in — cover your ears, Buddy — 'Hopefully, I'll be able to get sober'; and she can't stand the color orange. She's not fond of hearing me say that beer is food, which I'm afraid I've said several hundred times in her presence. She cries when she sees people snapping at their children in the grocery store. She hates all baseball teams that play indoors and she doesn't like it one little bit when people assume that God is male. So the part of AA that asks participants to look to "God as you understand *him*," just would not fly with my girl, and it's not gonna fly with me either. My wife has taught me a lot of things, and one of them is that the creative power of this universe is genderless. I've gotta say I like the idea of the power that shaped this gorgeous earth being beyond the ball and chain that is male and female, beyond the testosterone and the estrogen and the fistfights and the sanitary napkins, beyond the cold silence of the male and the hysterical tears of the female, beyond the penetrating and submitting to penetration, beyond it all, my patient listeners. I hope that answers your question."

It had been fun to drive by the billboard outside the station that featured Jay's face with the High on Wife hotline number beneath it. On the billboard he looked crazed, manic, like someone who should have been calling a hotline instead of answering one.

I'd felt happy hearing the testimonials of men who'd been inspired by Jay's example to put down the bong and the bottle to please their wives. Jay had a knack for dragging gory details from his on-air guests, and I thought this happened probably because it was impossible to feel weird next to Jay; he would always be a shade weirder. They confessed their infidelities, their sneaky, booze-inspired lies, their abuses of women and children. It was horrifying and riveting, the things these people said for all of Austin to hear, when I'd kept my troubles locked away in my heart from everyone but Darrah and the cat.

I was happy with the way Jay had started playing a lot of blues: Texas Alexander, Lil' Son Jackson, Lightning Hopkins.

I felt happy knowing that Jay was doing something for us, and I was afraid I'd show up at the station and find out that it was all just a big scam, one of Jay's many brilliant fundraising ideas. I was afraid I'd see him and immediately start my mental tally: half a joint, a six-pack of Shiner, a shot of gin. I'd been doing everything I could to avoid finding out the truth. I'd harassed my ballplayers until Coach had to call me into his office and tell me not to overdo it, that my job was safe even without Cory and Micah and Mike, that my job was safe even though our season had already started to crumble with a humiliating home series sweep at the hands of Southern Illinois, but there was always next year, right? Next year, with the recruits Coach was plotting to scoop up from these small-town Texas high schools where they really know how to hit the ball, by God, we'd certainly have a chance.

"Sure," I'd said, echoing Coach with all the emotion of a computer, "next year we'll be great."

On my seventh mile, when my lungs seemed to expand and deflate on their own, when it seemed it would take more effort to stop running than to keep going, I realized that beneath my fears about Jay's sincerity was this: I was afraid that when I saw him, I'd have to tell him about Heinz Fechtler. I was afraid it would fly out of my mouth, that my habit of telling him everything was too strong to break. I didn't want to break anything anymore. I wanted to mend.

But finally, I couldn't wait any longer, and on Saturday night, two days after Darrah had called, I drove down to the station. "Please let it be true," I said to the interior of my car. "Please let it be true." It had not been true many, many times before. Sometimes he'd started back on the same day he'd promised to stop. Other times, he'd tempted me with a day: "I'm having an alcohol-free day today, Buddy," he'd say, then by six o'clock he'd be mixing me a drink. For my twenty-seventh birthday he'd given me a year of sobriety. I remember, when he presented me with his promise, feeling glad that he'd given me some other presents as well (a new translation of Dostoyevsky's *The Demons* and a pair of small silver earrings) because I knew the year would soon shrink to six months, a month, a week. He lasted three weeks before he picked a fight with me and used it as an excuse to drink. "Happy birthday to me!" I sang in a screeching, poisonous voice as he slowly drained a bottle of gin. I couldn't help humming it, again, as I walked into the lobby.

The familiar lobby, with its walls of glass and gleaming floors of cold Spanish tile and plants that looked fake but weren't, had been transformed. About thirty people were stationed under a long, hand-painted banner that read TWENTY-SIX DAYS. Some of them lounged in sleeping bags, some sat in folding chairs, some sat cross-legged playing cards against the dark tiled floor. In the opposite corner of the lobby, near a large, potted cactus, someone had built a shrine to the victims of drunk drivers. Photos of the victims were arranged in a half circle, the inner circle filled with small candles, little plates of food, and various items that described the lives of the dead. My favorite item was a tiny Texas Rangers batting helmet, which I recognized because Jay and I had eaten ice cream out of helmets exactly like that one at a Rangers game; I remembered that we'd brought one home when Grace was a kitten, set it on his head, and took a photograph.

"Big changes around here," I said to Willie, the security guard, when I reached the elevator.

"Don't you know it," he said.

I pulled out my driver's license and he checked his list to make sure I was an approved visitor. Even though I'd been there countless times, even though I knew all about his wife, his son the fireman, and his daughter who had the basketball scholarship to Ole Miss and whose number, 32, Willie wore embroidered on the lapel of his uniform jacket, even though he knew all about me and had seen me both ecstatic and in tears, even though he knew damn well that I was the Wife of the High on Wife Marathon, he still paged carefully through his clipboard, still formally ticked off my name.

The music in the elevator was the radio station's: a very

old man mumbling "'Don't you leave me here/Don't you leave me here/But if you leave me here, oh darling dear/ Leave a dime for beer.'" When Jay's voice broke in, I kept riding the elevator, kept pushing random numbers that took me up and down, past the twenty-second floor again and again, just so I could hear my husband talk. "That was Texas bluesman Mance Lipscomb with 'Alabama Bound.' That's the blues, right there. You recognize the blues, don't you? Don't you? That's okay if you don't 'cause we're gonna talk about the blues right now. First thing you need to know is this: If you want to sing the blues, you better have the appropriate ride. Acceptable blues cars are Chevys, Cadillacs, and broke-down Fords. That's it. Forget Nissan, Geo, Lexus, Toyota, forget Mercedes. Again, that's a Chevrolet, a Cadillac, or a broke-down Ford, and the broke-down part is essential. Other acceptable blues transportation might be a southbound train, a Greyhound bus, a broke-down anything, any form of ramblin', or walkin' side by side with the devil. You do need to know that the devil is a vital part of the blues lifestyle. Ditch the shoes, or arrange to have your shoes stolen by your unsatisfied woman and you're even more legit. Mules are okay, too.

"Now what if you're overtaken by thirst, while you're cruising that lonesome, southbound highway on your mule? If you ask an unsatisfied woman for water and she gives you kerosene, you can be certain you've got the blues. But the main thing to remember here is that we do not have an extensive menu of acceptable blues beverages. Your options are, and listen closely, please: whiskey and an unsatisfied woman's bathwater. Microbrewed beer, organic carrot juice, sparkling mineral water, and decaf nonfat soy-milk lattes simply will not do. I'm not indulging in any of these blues beverages, though, gentles and nons, because I'm not going to *have* the blues when I reach the finish line of this hellish marathon to sobriety and my baby, my Buddy, my beloved Faith, a woman who would never substitute kerosene for water, is there waiting for me. Will she be there? Let's take that compelling question to Mississippi John Hurt with 'Ain't No Tellin.'"

By the first verse of Mississippi John's song I was standing next to Jay's booth, looking in. He had his head down in his arms, and he was perfectly still, and I realized that without marijuana and alcohol, his monologues had become draining. I felt sorry for him, and fascinated; it was rare to see Jay awake but not moving. Usually, if he was conscious, he remained in constant motion, tapping his foot, waving his arms, pacing frantically. I watched him for a moment, just for the strangeness of it, until he looked up and saw me. He smiled, and waved, even though we were only a few feet apart, then he slid off his headset and came out to me, his smile bigger with every step. Jay has a great smile, which I couldn't help but notice even in the worst moments. He has long, arching dimples on both sides of his mouth that you'd never know are there when he's not smiling. A nice surprise, every time.

"Hey, Buddy," he said, pulling me tight, then tighter.

"Hey, Buddy," I said. He kissed my cheek, my forehead, my other cheek.

"'Ain't no tellin' what she might do,'" sang Mississippi John Hurt.

"I'm really proud of you," I told him.

"Yeah? You don't think it's all a bunch of crap? I figured that's why you were staying away."

"I didn't want to get my hopes up again."

"That's my girl," he said.

"Can you blame me?"

"Not at all, Faith." I felt annoyed with him then. I felt he was using my name only to slap me in the face with its irony. I chose my words carefully.

"Jay, you've promised me more than a few times that you'd stop." What I meant was: You have promised me five fucking hundred times that you'd stop and you've broken every one of those promises wide open with a pickax.

"I know. I'm sorry, Buddy. I'm sorrier than I can say."

"Hey, where's Grace?" I said.

"Sleeping in the booth. Want to see him?" Jay said, cheering up with the change of subject. "I could show you some of my hate mail, too. I've been getting hate mail for talking about you too much on the air. Some of it's downright vitriolic. I love that word, don't you? Sounds like a drink. I'll have a vitriolic on the rocks."

"Yeah, I'd like to see him."

" 'She might shoot you/May cut and stab you too/ Ain't no tellin' what she might do.' "

"Hey, Buddy, would you consider going on the air? I mean, not right now, but sometime?"

"What for?"

"Just because people have heard so much about you. It might give people out there who are trying to get their spouses back some hope, you know. Not to assume I'm getting you back." He started blushing then, and pulled me close to hide it. But I knew what Jay's face looked like, blushing or not. If I never saw Jay's face again, I'd still know it. "I'm so sorry," he whispered, his mouth as close as possible to my ear. "I'm so sorry for what I've put you through."

Mississippi John Hurt had finished wondering what she might do and was singing about the candy man: "'All heard what sister Johnson said/She always takes a candy stick to bed.'"

"It's okay," I whispered back, and I let Jay lead me into the booth and I took our cat into my arms while Mississippi John Hurt sang, "'He sold some candy to sister Bad/The very next day she took all he had.'" Grace happily swiped the top of his head against the underside of my chin while Jay pressed a finger to his lips in the universal (as far as I know) gesture of silence, leaned into the microphone, and waited for Mississippi John to finish singing, "'His stick candy don't melt away/It just gets better, so the ladies say.'"

"Do you have the right to sing the blues?" Jay said. "The answer is yes if (a) your first name is the name of a physical deformity, your middle name is the name of a fruit, and your last name is the name of a Confederate leader, (b) either you or your woman can't be satisfied, (c) your unsatisfied woman stole your shoes, or (d) you've stabbed a man in St. Louis. If your first name is Kourtney with a *K,* you may not sing the blues even if you're shoeless, unsatisfied, *and* you've stabbed multiple men in St. Louis."

Blind Lemon Jefferson started to sing "'Peach orchard mama, you swore that nobody picked your fruit but me.'"

"Okay," Jay said. "We're free for about fifteen minutes."

"'I found three kid men shaking down your peaches free.'"

"Great stuff, Jay," I said.

"Thanks, Buddy. So how are you? How's the team? I've missed you like crazy."

"The team's pitiful. We're already into the maybe-next-year talk."

"Yeah, well, maybe next year, Buddy."

"Very funny. So how does it feel, being sober?" Jay was clearly sober, but still I held my breath, still afraid he'd say *Oh, I'm not really sober, it's just good publicity for the radio station. I've really cut down, though. Things are going to be different, Buddy, I promise.*

But instead he said, "Most of the time I just want to wrap my lips around a bong, if you know what I mean. Like I'm hyperalert and I just want to come down so I can rest, like I don't really *want* to notice every last detail of everyone's face — except yours, of course — like reality is getting kind of *intrusive*, you know, and I'd just like to take a big toke or a drink and beat it back a ways. But it feels good to be doing something for you, Buddy, something for us. That part of it feels great. How have you been, Buddy? You been okay?"

"I guess so," I said, starting to cry a little.

He rolled his chair close to mine and pulled me onto his lap. Grace slid to the floor and swirled around our feet, purring. Jay shoved the microphone part of his headset away from his mouth and kissed me, a long, sweet kiss, long enough for a hundred wild hopes to rouse themselves in my mind: a shared bed, a blooming rosebush, a dear little yard planted with clover and encased in a picket fence — a picket fence! I've been crazy enough to dream of a picket fence! — a white picket fence with some sort of flowering vine twisting through it, kiss after kiss after kiss, long Saturdays spent fixing all the things on our house we'd always meant to fix (the crooked baseboard in the kitchen, the rotten windowsills in back, the door that won't shut right when it rains), elaborate celebrations of all our little anniversaries (our engagement, our wedding, the day we first used the word *love*, and especially January 25, the anniversary of our wonderful first kiss), all of them celebrated with Jay awake and present and with me, baths taken not for cleanliness but because we want to be together in a body of water, extended Sundays spent reading the *New York Times* and eating little chocolate pastries and drinking good coffee from huge, warm cups, kiss after kiss after kiss, all of those kisses exchanged with no alteration of our body chemistry other than what flows through the veins when two people are in love. We kissed for a long time, long enough for Blind Willie Johnson to finish singing about his marriage to Jesus, long enough for Taj Mahal to swear he'd never seen no whiskey but the blues made him sloppy drunk, long enough for Lightning Hopkins to tell about Katie Mae and the oil wells in her backyard. After that Bill Wilbur started in with " 'My babe, my babe, sure been good to me.' " I slid back to my own chair, Grace reinstated himself on my lap, and I held my husband's hands tightly in my own.

"Hey, Buddy," Jay said. "You been seeing anyone else? No, never mind. That's not what I meant to say. That's not you at all, I know. What I meant was, are we still married?"

Something had changed in my face in the seconds after Jay said *someone else* and before I could say, "Of course we're still married," and I gripped his hands tighter as he stared at me. I held his hands so tight my arms shook.

"What the hell?" he said.

"Jay," I said, "I had waited and waited for you to call me, to tell me you were quitting, and then I turned on your show and you were having people call in with their hangover cures. I just couldn't take it anymore. It was just that one night, and I wish it had never happened, and if you'd given me even a slight hint that you were considering getting sober, it wouldn't have happened. I hope you can forgive me."

The horrible words *my babe, my babe, sure been good to me* pelted us like hail.

"Yeah, I hope I can too," Jay said. He looked at me coldly, then jerked his hands from mine and started flipping through a stack of CDs.

"You mean you don't know if you can or not?"

"Yeah, I don't know."

"You mean that after everything I've put up with from you, you don't know if you can forgive me for one mistake?"

"You fucked someone else, Faith!" he yelled. Then he abruptly cut off Bill Wilbur's song, right in the middle of the verse that ran "I can ask her for whiskey/She give me cherry wine/Don't you wish your woman/Would treat you good like mine." The station was broadcasting dead air.

"Jay!" I said. "Put something on!"

"You want to talk? You want to tell my listeners you went and fucked some other guy?" He wrenched the microphone from his headset and shoved it in my face until its rough mesh pressed against my lips. I stood up, toppling the cat, and ran out of there.

Your Cheating Heart

After I ran out of the station, away from the cold black head of that microphone and Jay's snarled-up face, Jay set up the system to play Ray Charles's version of "Your Cheating Heart" over and over. I heard the first strains as I rushed out of the elevator, past Willie and the shrine to victims of drunk drivers and past Jay's groupies in their brightly colored sleeping bags. I let Ray continue to sing as I drove; he cycled through the song four or five times before I turned the radio off.

I drove without knowing where I was going, with no map in my head of how to get to the little house with a picket fence and a sober husband. I thought I'd even settle for a different kind of fence, a split-rail fence or one of those weird bamboo jobs you buy in a big roll, barbed wire or chainlink. Just give me the sober husband.

I drove by Darrah's, hoping she might be up late with the baby, but her house was a dark shape on the dark street. I thought of the terrible things Darrah used to say about *breeders,* as she once called people who have babies, thought of her once-constant ranting about abortion rights and birth control in the water ("It's only dumb-asses who drink tap water, right? So we dose the municipal water supplies with birth control, and the gene pool improves immediately; you have the intelligent, bottled-water drinkers breeding, and the masses can't conceive"). I thought about Darrah's gorgeous child. Lucy had been born by C-section, just lifted right out of my friend, without the wrinkles, the redness, and the misshaped skull of babies who have to fight their way out of the birth canal. She had been perfect from the start. I thought of the terrible things Darrah had once said about marriage, that it was a tool of the state, that she wouldn't be caught dead participating in such a patriarchal system. Now she had a husband and a daughter and a Ford Explorer filled with baby gear. She raved about something called a Diaper Genie. I wanted to go bang down her door and slip into her body and own every part of her life.

I drove on through Darrah's neighborhood, past all the dark little houses with happy people sleeping inside them. I tried and could not call up Heinz Fechtler's face, his touch, an unknown language whispered in my ear. I tried and couldn't remember what had driven me to walk into his bedroom, to take off my clothes and do things I had vowed to do only with my husband. I thought of my mother, of the silence between us, of the things she'd written about how to grow tomatoes from seed: "Seedlings," she advised, "like infants, require far more attention than the full-grown plant, or, as the case may be, the full-grown child. Provide tomato seedlings with at least fourteen to sixteen hours of light per day. Use cool white fluorescent tubes, kept two to four inches above the plants. Keep the soil moist, but not soggy. Talk to them about happy things. Avoid sudden, harsh sounds, and rock and roll music."

I found myself parked in front of our house, the house where I'd lived with Jay. It's a small stone house, just two bedrooms and one bath, but it has a deep front porch, deep enough for two hammocks to swing side by side. Jay and I had had some sweet times in our hammocks, talking on the dark porch, reaching our fingers through the netting every so often to touch. We'd bought them in Mexico, on our first Christmas together, from a vendor on the beach in Puerto Angel. *Cerveza, por favor,* was the first thing Jay learned to say in Spanish. I taught him *te amo, te quiero, te extraño mucho.*

"When the seedlings show their first set of true leaves," my mother had written, "begin to thump their stems once or twice a day with a gentle flick of the index finger. This will cause the seedlings to become sturdy and stout. Tell them, as you're thumping, that you expect them to become sturdy and stout. Tell them that they are destined to produce many gorgeous, sweet, juicy tomatoes. Tomatoes, like all children and some adults, respond well to having something expected of them."

I had expected, told, and thumped, and still things had gone horribly wrong.

I drove back to the dorms, punched in the wrong security code twice, and finally ran up the stairs, the disembodied voice of Ray Charles blaring in my head. *What do you know about it?* I wanted to scream. I locked the door to my room, ripped off my clothes, yanked the covers tight over my head, and raced toward sleep and the phone call that came in the middle of the night. Jay's voice was his own, with a thousand hairline cracks.

"Buddy," he said.

"What is it?" My voice sounded loud in the darkness of my room.

"Buddy, please come over. I need you to come over right now."

"Home?"

"Please, Buddy."

"Are you still mad at me? Can you forgive me now?"

"Yeah, I can forgive you." He was crying by then. I wanted to think he was crying over me, that he'd had enough of our troubles and was ready to roll up his sleeves and help me fix it all. But I think I already knew it was something else pulling the tears from him, something outside the edges of his love for me, and I drove home cautiously, through the yellow blinking stoplights and the empty streets.

Jay was just out of the shower, a towel slung around his waist; he smelled of toothpaste and soap over a steady, low throb of alcohol. He wrapped his arms around me and I felt the heat misting off his bare skin.

"Hey, Buddy," he said. "Buddy, I've done a terrible thing."

"You drank," I said.

"I had a wreck, Faith," he said, pulling me tighter to keep this news from jerking me out of his arms.

"You what?"

"I think I might have hurt someone." It took me a second to realize that the someone wasn't me.

He told me how he'd left the station, walked down the back stairs and across the parking lot to his truck, his darling little Toyota truck in which we'd had some truly exceptional makeout sessions, and drove to a bar. He told me he had a few shots. He drank until the bartender cut him off. He told me how the Rangers game was playing on the bar TV, how he joined the other men there in making derogatory comments about the Rangers' decimated pitching staff. Jay commented to the other drunks that although the word *decimated* is often used to mean "demolished" or "destroyed," it literally means "reduced to one-tenth of its former number." This is the kind of thing he usually restrained himself from saying in bars, the kind of comment that tended to make other men want to edge away from him or pound his head in.

He told me how, when the bartender was no longer willing to trade alcohol for Jay's money, Jay walked outside, started up his truck, and pulled out onto South Congress. At the West Mary intersection, the one that's hardly ever busy, Jay's right turn got loose and he slammed into the driver's side of a red Honda Civic. It happened right in front of a house we used to drive by all the time, where a goat roamed the tiny front yard. It's one of the things we liked about South Austin, the fact that someone could keep a goat in his yard, right in the middle of the city, and no one would raise much of a fuss about it.

"You know, the house with the goat," Jay said, unnecessarily.

Jay kept on driving. He drove to a pay phone at the corner of First and Mary and called in the wreck. He made his voice high, like a woman's, gave the voice a twangy, East Texas accent. He told the emergency operator she'd better get someone down there to have a look-see. Then he drove home, shut the truck up in our garage, and called me at the dorms.

"No, Jay," I said.

He pulled away from me then and started tearing through his closet for something to wear.

"It was like this," he said in the East Texas female voice. He pulled on a pair of khakis and a white shirt.

"Jay, we have to go back there! We have to make sure that person is okay! We have to call the hospitals, or the police, or something!" His face was wild. He had buttoned his shirt wrong. I unbuttoned it for him and started all over. My hands shook around the slim buttons. "Jay, how much time do you think has passed since you . . . since you called in the wreck?"

"I don't know, Buddy. I couldn't tell you."

Before I could say anything else he pulled away from me, two buttons still undone, picked up the phone, and called Rodney, his technician.

"Yeah, man," he said, "it's Evers. Sorry I had to blow outta there. I got really sick all of a sudden, some kind of withdrawal thing, I think. Yeah, I puked my brains out for a couple of hours and I feel okay now. I'm on my way back. Don't worry, man, I won't get my germs on you. You remember that doctor I had on the other night? She said something like this might happen as I start to release my toxins, and I'm sure I have a few of those. Toxins, I mean. Yeah, well, see you in a few. Yeah, man, leave it on until I get back and I'll do a call-in hour or something. Cool." Tears coated Jay's face, but his voice was steady; it was his radio voice, ready to please.

"Jay . . . are you still drunk?"

"Maybe she'll be okay, Buddy. I think it was a she. I'm not sure. Could you take me to the station and we'll figure it out from there?"

"It, Jay? You think *it* was a *she*? You ran into a *person*, and you don't even know if she's dead or alive!"

"I know!" he yelled. "You think I don't know that?"

"You smell like a distillery," I said, my voice full of an angry coldness I didn't recognize. "You smell terrible."

He tore off his clothes and lurched back to the shower. I leaned against the bathroom doorway and watched his wet, blurred figure. I started to realize that everything we had been through so far was nothing compared with what lay ahead, and I wanted to throw up.

"When your tomatoes begin setting fruit," my mother had written,

> give thanks to whomever you enjoy thanking for such things. Take your packet of tomato seeds from the fridge, where you should have been storing it all this time, and pour one of the tiny, pale chips into your hand. Look at the seed. Look up at the huge plants that are working hard to make you one of the most delicious things you could ever hope to put in your mouth. If you feel a deep, curving wave of awe and respect crashing over you, or if you feel even a small ripple of same, know that you have a good heart. Know that you're fine.

I closed my eyes and tried to breathe, tried to stop the universe from branching out with possibilities: I saw us as very old people with the secret of the accident still caught between us, a bulky mess between us and getting around it like trying to make love in winter clothing, layers of wool and humid turtlenecks and the effort of getting through it all to the cool, tight skin of the matter. I saw us in our forties with a child playing on our floor, Jay's time served and a new life started and with it the right to teach a new human being what it means to tell the truth. I saw that damn picket fence with flowering vines wound through it, trumpet vines and morning glories and exotic things recommended by my mother. By then I was accustomed to steering my mind sharply away from my picket-fence dream, and I did so, and I saw a vast stretch of lonely, sad, weird days, nights when I would eat cafeteria food with my boys (sloppy joes! mac and cheese! muscle-building protein drinks!) and long for a kitchen, a table, and someone to sit across from me, never mind the stupid picket fence.

I don't know how we walked out of our house, locked the door behind us, opened the heavy doors to my Chevelle, and stepped in. I don't know how I found a voice to say, "Jay, let's go back there, right now. The police are probably still there. You could just tell them. Tell them you had to leave to call for help, and then you wanted to get your wife be- cause . . . because you wanted someone sober to drive you back there. Something like that." Jay's eyes were closed. I couldn't see his smile lines in the dark, or the vertical lines in his cheeks that opened to dimples when he smiled, but I knew where it all was. "Jay," I said.

"I know, I know," he said. "It's the right thing to do."

"And it's our only chance," I said.

He opened his eyes and turned toward me, then he slid across the seat and kissed me. I don't know how I managed to enjoy that kiss, but I did enjoy it, that harsh, long kiss: lips to lips, teeth to teeth, not a thought of a damn picket fence anywhere near me.

"Should we go?" I whispered when he'd pulled back.

"Yeah," he said. "What do you think I'm going to do to you now? Become a fugitive from the law?"

"I don't know," I said.

I started the motor, a roar in the quiet night, made a U-turn, and drove toward Mary Street. When we were only a few blocks away I said, "Do you want me to go with you, to the police station?"

"I think I'd rather you go back to the radio station and tell them," Jay said. "They're fucked in a way, you know, because everyone took off for vacation when I started the marathon. No one's around except Miss Perfect."

"The Mistress."

"Yeah. I have some prerecorded stuff but I doubt they'll want to play it, after this comes out. Tell Ron . . . tell everyone I'm sorry." We were almost there then; I could almost see the bumpy roll of the police lights.

"I will," I said.

Then we were there, and I pulled over behind one of four police cars and I could see ahead of them the dark ruin of the car Jay had hit. The fat owner of the goat sat on his front steps smoking a cigarette, his legs spread wide to make room for his belly. I didn't see the goat, or an ambulance.

A cop walked back to our car and rapped on my window and said, when I'd rolled it down, "You folks are gonna need to move along, now."

The red, white, and blue lights waved across my vision like a watery flag.

"Yes, sir," I said, and I backed the car up a few feet and then pulled a U-turn. I tried to keep my speed down as I drove away, but I drove faster, and faster, until I couldn't make myself stop for a red light and I ran it, quickly glancing both ways but not really seeing anything except the glare of my own tears. I pulled over in the dark parking lot of a Mexican restaurant where Jay and I had sometimes gone for breakfast.

"Hey, it was orange," Jay said.

"Sorry."

"What are you doing, Faith?"

"I can't stand to let you go," I cried. He slid over, across the shiny cloth seat, and worked his shoulder under my wet face. "I'm tired of being away from you," I said into his shirt. "I'm so tired of it."

"Faith," Jay whispered, and his voice was barely there, his voice was worn thin from everything that had happened, from the knowledge that we had been apart for a long, long time, far longer than the weeks since I'd walked out of our house, we'd been apart all those hours when Jay had been drunk and then unconscious, when he'd been hung over and I'd been angry and silent, or angry and nagging, all those nights when we'd slept in the same bed like two people who didn't even know each other, like people who in the morning look at the face beside them and have to struggle for a name, for an idea of where their car keys might be.

"Buddy," Jay whispered, and he lifted my head and brushed my hair back from my face, hooked long strands of it around my ears and ran the back of his hand along my cheek. Beyond Jay's face, piñatas crowded the restaurant window: parrots, sombreros, a monstrous spike-heeled shoe. "Buddy," Jay said, "you're always with me. Do you hear me? You're always with me. Without you I'm nothing. Without you I'm a big pile of dirt. I'm something smelly in your mom's compost pile. I'm roadkill. I'm toxic waste. You're with me, girl, whether you want to be or not."

"Why didn't you call me all that time?"

"I don't know, Buddy. I started cooking on the marathon thing and it took a while to convince R.J. and the board and to get the thing organized and I just . . . I wanted it to be a surprise. I wanted to just blow you away with something elegant, something amazing, something you never expected. I should have told you, though. You were suffering and I should have told you."

I cried in Jay's arms for a long time, and he kissed the top of my head and whispered little things. After a while he said, "Faith, I know I have absolutely no right to ask you this, but I have to give it a shot."

"What's that?"

"Will you wait for me, until this is all over? Will you still be my wife when it's over?"

I can't honestly say if what I felt was love or a perverse desire for a challenge, but it felt enough like love that I said, "Yes, I will."

Jay covered every inch of my face with kisses and then he said, "Buddy, let's go back."

"Yeah," I said. "Okay."

I started the car. As my headlights bloomed on the restaurant window, I saw an even bigger piñata, one shaped like a baseball. The stitching was strange, the lines of it not quite shapely enough, but it was definitely a baseball.

"Look," I said to Jay. He saw it and smiled.

"Hey, why do the O's suck so much this year?" he said. "They're the same team on paper as last year."

"Except for their manager," I said. "You can't do anything without a good manager. Helps to have a closer, too. It's still so early, though. You never know what might happen."

I cried even harder, and Jay kissed away the tears as fast

as they came, then he gave my forehead a last kiss and I put the car in gear and drove back to the accident scene.

The same policeman who'd told me to move along walked up to the car and said, "Ma'am, I thought I told you . . ."

Jay reached over and gave my hand a last squeeze and then he was out of the car and the cop met him at the front of the hood and I couldn't hear what they were saying, but the cop motioned for the other cops and they all started to walk toward the car and then the first one, the one who'd told us to go, pulled Jay's hands behind his back and circled them with handcuffs. Jay looked down at the hood, although he could have looked at me if he'd wanted to. I thought maybe the police would want to talk to me, and maybe they should have, but they left me alone and led Jay toward one of their cars and I sat there with the motor running for a few minutes, until two police cars and then the one holding Jay had pulled away and there were just two policemen left to supervise the tow-truck driver whose job it was to drag off the crumpled Honda, then I pulled another U-turn and drove to the radio station and sat in the parking lot for a few minutes.

As soon as I'd turned off the motor, I felt like I was just there to visit Jay, that I'd walk in and he'd greet me with his huge, dimpled smile, that I'd sit there on his lap listening to him babble over the air about sobriety. In spite of everything I'd seen that night, I found it almost impossible to believe Jay had done what he had done.

That's not what Jay does, I thought. *He doesn't get drunk and run people down. He gets drunk and paces around our house reading me random paragraphs from novels he likes until the whole living room floor is covered in books. He gets drunk and talks for half an hour about how some Cormac McCarthy* novel is *"like Faulkner on acid." He gets drunk and rants about how he wants to make love to me for hours, how he won't be happy until he's delivered to me about eight hours of nonstop pleasure, then he passes out before he can get my first button undone. He gets drunk and high and then gets the munchies and makes a wreck of the kitchen trying to bake chocolate chip cookies, and the cookies don't turn out because he was so stoned he added four cups of flour instead of two, so he has to order a pizza to satisfy his stoned hunger since the cookies are like doorstops and he orders another six-pack with the pizza and I try not to say "Haven't you had enough?" I try to concentrate on the book I'm reading, I focus on each word until a string of words becomes a sentence, until the sentences become a paragraph, until I forget about the beer delivery and my wreck of a kitchen and how Jay will be completely passed out before he even thinks of cleaning it up. I think of how I'd like to leave the mess for him to clean up in the morning, when he's hung over, but if I leave it hundreds of ants will march right through the back door and will dance all over my counter and I won't be able to sleep knowing the sink is filled with dirty, ant-covered dishes, knowing my sink is a beacon for every ant in the neighborhood. So I will clean it myself, and I'll be angrier with every dish I scrub.*

I sat in the car in the dark parking lot of the radio station and thought about the sick joke of our lives. I thought about how I had spent years trying to improve Jay's behavior and then at the last minute had almost steered him sharply away from doing the right and honest thing. I felt like a huge failure of a person, like someone who had no right at all to lecture athletes about character, about how to channel their tempers into their on-field performances, about setting a good example for the youth of Austin, Texas. *Failure is a big part of the game,* I told myself. *Failure is a big part of the game.* I thought about how I would have given anything to be home with Jay right then, to be righteously pissed off about a bunch of dirty dishes and a husband passed out on the couch. I looked back almost fondly at those angry versions of myself, at that woman snapping a dish towel and flinging down the sponge, as if she were a little girl staging a temper tantrum over nothing, over a spilled ice cream cone or a broken toy, as if her anger shone as beautifully as her most spectacular smile.

When News Breaks Out We Break In

Rodney, the technician, took the news with a deep breath and a short little sigh and a matter-of-fact "We're fucked." Then he got busy making clips of Jay's voice until he pieced together enough to make my disembodied husband say, "How about a call-in hour, dear ones? Your views, my ears, and the subject is . . ." Then Rodney made Ray Charles sing "Your Cheating Heart."

"Phone's been ringing off the freakin' hook about that song," Rodney said. "I guess I'm gonna have to wake up Ron, see what he wants to do. You wanta get this cat outta here?"

I scooped up the cat and the half-full bag of cat food and didn't listen to the station all the way back to the dorms because Grace's standard car howl was about all I could take, but all night long I stayed frozen in my bed, waiting for snippets of Jay's voice, hoping for it like we hope for rain in August, even though everything's already dried up by then, even though it's too late for a rain to help matters.

"Well if you want to know what I think," a female caller said, "I think we've set ourselves up to be cheated on by constructing these cheatable institutions. Like if there were no taxes people wouldn't be able to cheat on them, and if we didn't have marriage, cheating wouldn't be such a big deal. Because don't you think we're all really bisexual at heart? Don't you think we're really just cheating ourselves by limiting ourselves to these monogamous heterosexual relationships anyway?"

I wondered what would happen to all those barely sober people in the station's lobby. I wondered if KXAL would have to give back all the money that had been contributed. I wondered if that person who'd been in the Honda was dead or alive.

"Okay, this is my definition of cheating: If you do less with someone else than you do with your partner, it's not cheating. But if you do the same or more, it's cheating. Like if you have sex with your partner and you just kiss someone else but don't have sex, it doesn't count. You get what I'm saying?"

I wondered how we would tell our parents. I thought of the time I had stood in Jay's mother's kitchen in Cambridge and said something about how Jay certainly liked to drink, how she had cut me off immediately and said, "Faith, men drink." Then she had walked out of the kitchen to the outside deck and started watering the geraniums, even though we were in the middle of cooking a lobster dinner, even though the water was boiling and the lobsters were waving in slow motion from the ice-filled sink.

"I have insomnia which is the only reason I've turned the radio on in the first place," said a shivery old voice, "and I just want to say that cheating is wrong and there's no two ways about it and all the discussion in the world isn't going to change that. I think we should end this right here and get back to that nice young man who's trying to stop being a drunk."

"KXAL, you're on the air," Rodney had my husband say. I had the feeling Rodney was enjoying his chance to be king of the station, that perhaps he had put off calling Ron, the station manager, that he looked forward to staying up all night manipulating Jay's voice. He could have just played music, after all.

"I cheat every chance I get and I don't worry about it at all. That's what condoms are for."

I thought of my own parents, of what I would say to them. I hadn't said anything at all to my mother since I'd stormed out of her garden on that Houston trip, and Daddy and I relied on Mother for news of each other. I wondered if he even knew that Mother and I weren't speaking, or if Mother had just continued to tell him that *Faith says hello, Henry. She says for me to hug your neck.*

"Yeah, I just want to say that people who cheat are kind of pathetic. Kind of sleazy and pathetic. And if there are any guys out there who don't happen to be sleazy and pathetic, and who have the guts to make a commitment and stick to it, my name is Kelly Sackheim and I'm in the book."

Perhaps this new crisis would be enough to startle Mother's focus away from her giant tomato. Maybe she'd come to Austin to be with me while Jay and I went through whatever we were going to have to go through. Maybe she'd let her tomato rot on the vine while she helped me through it all. Perhaps she'd come stay with me at the house, and help me get a little garden of my own started.

"Can I just say something? Two years ago my boyfriend

cheated on me with my best friend and naturally I stopped speaking to both of them, but you want to know the worst thing about it? It wasn't losing my boyfriend. It was losing my friend. I miss her like I've never missed him. And I'm not a lesbian or anything. But I can hardly remember his face and I remember everything she and I ever said to each other."

I thought of why I like baseball better than football: because baseball isn't regulated by a clock, because each game has an organic form; each game is as fast or slow or lumpy or sleek as the players make it.

"All you people who think it's okay to cheat haven't looked at your Bibles lately, which by the way the Bible is the best-selling book of all time and I think that speaks for itself."

I edged in and out of sleep all night, my little radio close to my head, until it was almost six in the morning and Rodney's voice started to read off the local news. "When news breaks out we break in," Jay had been obliged to say at the start and finish of each news broadcast. We agreed that it was a ridiculous motto, as the news was read at certain scheduled times and never involved any "breaking in."

"City Council is expected to vote today on a possible widening of the Lamar Street bridge that has some South Austin residents worried about an increase in traffic through their neighborhoods. Northbound I-35 is backed up from the downtown exits to William Cannon due to a jackknifed semi blocking all but the right-hand lane just south of MLK. Twenty-nine-year-old Austinite Alice Jamison was the victim of a fatal accident in South Austin last night. Austin police haven't yet determined whether alcohol was a factor in the two-car crash, which occurred shortly after one o'clock A.M. More of this gorgeous spring weather to come, with highs expected to be in the upper eighties all week with clear, sunny skies. Current temperature is seventy-two degrees. When news breaks out we break in."

Sobah

The morning after the wreck, when Jay was still in county jail with a bail so high it sounded like lottery winnings ("I'm a killer, Buddy. What'd you expect?" he'd say later that day), I was supposed to meet Dick Walston, the football coach, for a recruiting breakfast. We were to woo a boy from Abilene who at that time was the fastest sprinter in the nation, but whose GPA/SAT combination wasn't yet high enough to make him eligible to play for us.

"Another brain trust," I told the cat as I struggled out of bed. "And if he does boost his scores, we'll probably lose him to Florida."

I cried in the shower for a while and then I picked out a flowered dress to wear; Coach wanted me to help convince this boy's parents that our campus would provide their darling with the equivalent of a small-town atmosphere — why, the UT campus was really no different from a town like Abilene! — as opposed to that den of iniquity he'd face in Florida. I was supposed to represent the small-town school-teacher, the old maid in a flowered dress who would mold their child into an outstanding citizen. I buttoned up my dress, twisted my hair into a bun, and phoned the radio station at a few minutes before seven. I figured I would never need the advice of the Mistress more than I did right then. I figured it was finally time to call.

Jeffrey, the morning technician, took my call. He wouldn't have known my voice — it was really the night staff that knew me — but I put on a fake voice anyway, a brassy, small-town Texas voice. I pictured myself with big hair and boots for which several reptiles had been sacrificed. I visualized myself wearing a leather belt with my name stitched on the back. I imagined myself in skin-tight Wranglers. I saw my eyelashes heavy and rough with mascara. At the last minute I wished I'd chosen a southern accent instead, something from the Mississippi Delta, the voice of a woman who owns a porcelain magnolia blossom, pillows needlepointed with cotton bolls, dark, smoky paintings that depict men hunting.

"I can't guarantee that she'll take your call," Jeffrey said. "We're already pretty backed up this morning. But if you could give me the basics of your situation I'll put you in the pool and we'll see what we can do."

"Why would she maybe not take my call?" She had to take my call!

"Like say if we have another caller with your same situation. We don't want to put two callers on in one segment with the same situation."

"I seriously doubt that anyone else has my same situation," I said.

"You'd be surprised. So what is it?"

I told him the bones of it, changing a few details. I called myself Tammy. I said it was a pedestrian who'd been hit. I said the person had been hospitalized, not killed. I said my husband was forty-five years old and had promised me on our tenth wedding anniversary, two weeks before the incident, that he would get sober. If I had gone the Mississippi Delta route, I could have said *sobah*.

"Yeah, okay," he said, not willing to admit to the uniqueness of my dilemma but unable to hide the surprise in his voice. "I'm going to put you on hold now."

The hold message was the humming part of Taj Mahal's "Texas Woman" overlaid with Jay's voice promoting the High on Wife Marathon, urging me to call up the station and give away all my money. I wondered why they hadn't changed it yet; I imagined Jay's voice suddenly interrupted with a booming news bulletin about what he had done. I hummed along with Taj until Jeffrey came back and informed me that the Mistress was going to take my call but that it would be in the second half hour of that hour of the program.

"Great," I said, stretching the word to the maximum possible number of syllables.

"No use of the f-word on the air," he informed me. "And please keep the volume on your radio completely down or turn it off altogether. And when it's your turn, try to state your situation as concisely as you possibly can."

"Got it," I said.

I stretched out on my bed, trying not to wrinkle my small-town flowered teacher dress, and set the phone far enough away from me so Jay's sales pitch was blurry and indistinct, so that it could have been anyone, saying anything. I concentrated on the Mistress, who was impatiently listening to a woman's story of how she had married because she was pregnant but ended up miscarrying the baby and divorcing after three months. What she needed to know was, see, it's like this, um, should she give the wedding presents back?

"And why wouldn't you give them back after this absurdly short marriage, after this *joke* of a marriage?"

"'Cause, um, I got some really cool stuff."

"Cool stuff!" the Mistress roared. "Get your immature little butt down to the stationery store, buy a box of cards, and write the following on each one. Are you writing this down? I don't want you to miss this."

"Okay, let me get a pen," the girl said. After some rummaging-around noises, a dog bark, and a yelled "Hold on!," she came back, panting.

"'Dear so-and-so," the Mistress said, "thank you for the lovely gift. I appreciate your taking the time to acknowledge my marriage. It is unfortunate that I did not spend an equal amount of time contemplating the covenant I was entering. In light of my recent divorce, I would like to return your thoughtful gift and to apologize for the inconvenience I caused you.'"

"What was that last part? After 'thoughtful gift'?"

"I don't do repeats," the Mistress said. "Ask someone who's a better listener."

By the time she took my call, she had straightened out a couple who couldn't decide whether to put their new baby in day care or sacrifice some income so one of them could stay home ("This is like choosing between mother's milk and formula. One's the real thing and one's not"), a man whose wife was a crack user ("You knew this about her before you married her and don't tell me you didn't. You married her anyway because you had the arrogance to think you could change her. You've got a big fat slice of humble pie on your plate, buster, and I want you to start eating"), and a woman whose fiancé wanted her to convert to Catholicism but she just couldn't quite believe the teachings of the Church and should she convert anyway ("Listen closely: You have to believe it in your heart or else you will be living a lie. You will be acting out a lie every time you take part in the rituals of the Church. And I believe that lying in one area of your life makes it easier to lie in other areas, so this conversion-without-faith idea could not possibly be good for your marriage, no matter how much your Catholic boyfriend wants you to join his little cult. It will lead to bumlike behavior on your part, and I don't think you want to be a bum, do you?").

While the potentially Catholic caller whined a little more, I drifted into a fantasy in which I would change my identity and disappear to some city with a major league ball club, get a job as an usher in the ballpark, and spend the rest of my years growing into a crusty old woman who knows *The Baseball Encyclopedia* by heart and relentlessly heckles opposing team batters.

When it was my turn to speak, when the Mistress said, "Tammy, what can I help you with?" I felt far more nervous than I'd thought I would. My fake accent trembled and quavered. I took a deep breath and said, "Mistress, I've been married ten years to a wonderful forty-five-year-old man with whom I'm very much in love, but we have a terrible dilemma."

"I'll decide if your husband's wonderful or not, so spare me the adjectives, please."

"Okay, well, our problem is that he has had a drinking

problem for several years and it recently escalated into him driving drunk, hitting a pedestrian, and putting this person in the hospital."

"Oh, great!" the Mistress yelled. "I hope the bum's in prison where he belongs!"

"Yes, ma'am, he is, but I'm wondering if, you know, if I should stay with him, if we have any chance of continuing our marriage and putting this behind us." Of course, I had already promised Jay that I *would* wait for him, that we *would* put this behind us, but still I felt compelled to grope for some reinforcement, and I held my breath as I waited for her answer. My unasked questions swirled in my head: Why had I driven away from the accident scene? Why had I gone to bed with Heinz? Why had I acted like such a bum?

"Dear," the Mistress said. "I think you've spent enough time being married to a bum. My advice for you is to look within yourself and figure out what it is about *you* that allows you to be attracted to such a person. Is it just plain stupidity or something more complex? If you can figure that out, you will be giving yourself quite a gift. In the meantime, forget him and move on. Thanks for your call."

"But wait —" I said to the buzz of the disconnected line. I wanted to say *But you don't really know him. You don't know how sweet he can be, the letters he can write — you've never read one of Jay's letters. You don't know how it sounds when he calls me Buddy, you just don't know the person he is, and I know this accident thing looks bad, I know it is bad, but you should have seen him on our wedding day: When the preacher had finished his long questioning litany of do-you this and do-you that, do-you do-you do-you, when it was time for Jay to say*

"I do," he said instead, so solemnly, *"It is my highest calling."*
That's *the kind of person he is, he had* thought *about our wedding vows, he had thought up his own darling answer instead of
droning out his part of a script, and* that's *why I want to keep
loving him.*

The Mistress had once said this to a woman who didn't
want her husband to press charges against an employee who
had embezzled from their company: "Why do you think you
identify with a bad person? I'll tell you: It's because you
want to be let off the hook as well."

Was that me? Did I love Jay because he offered me absolutely no competition, because I would always seem more
together than he was? Did I love Jay the way I loved peren-
nially losing baseball teams: the Cubs, the Red Sox, the
much-maligned Texas Rangers? Did I love having something
to cheer for without the worry of maintaining a winner?
Had I been able to drive away from the accident because it
still wasn't nearly as bad as what Jay had done?

I had to leave for the recruiting breakfast ten minutes
after I hung up the phone, but I wanted to listen to one last
call. I wanted to forget about all the things I had to do that
morning, the things that would go undone while I went to
breakfast and then to the county jail: I needed to decorate
the study lounge and pick up the cake for Micah's going-
away party that would be held that night; I needed to sit in
on the eight o'clock Russian lit class that was giving Leo
Rhodes fits. But I had the elements of Russian literature
down — one heartbreak after another, either political or
personal — well enough that I could afford to skip the class,
well enough that I could afford to slouch on my bed and lis-

ten to the Mistress decide who was a bum and who wasn't for a little while longer. I closed my eyes. My gift to myself, for the moment, would be this: I would slump on the bed, wrinkling my flowered dress and pretending, for just a very few minutes, that none of this had happened.

Darn Close

Coach Walston had scheduled breakfast at a place where the menu was stamped with cartoon pigs who advertised themselves for eating and where the waitress, when Coach ordered the egg, ham, and sausage plate, drawled, "How you want yer yellers?"

Coach smiled at the potential recruit and his parents, as if to say *See, Austin's practically a small town! How could your son go wrong in a town where the waitresses say "How you want yer yellers"?*

The restaurant was not piping Jay's station over its dusty speakers; instead, it played country, all heartbreak and cheatin' and lo-o-onesome nights.

"Faith here," Coach was saying as he clapped a big hand down on my shoulder, "she and her staff keep our boys on top of their classes. We don't see any reason why a great athlete can't be a great student as well, and Faith not only keeps these boys eligible for play, she actually makes sure they learn something. Right, Faith?"

"Right," I said.

"'You promised me homemade biscuits but I got frozen waffles instead,'" someone wailed over the radio.

"Three national championships," Coach was saying. "And we came darn close to a fourth, if it hadn't been for a fumbled punt. Right, Faith?"

"Darn close," I said.

The boy and his parents looked back and forth from Coach to me, as if we were a tennis match. The boy's father wore a camouflage cowboy hat I could hardly take my eyes off; it had exactly the opposite effect of what's traditionally intended by camouflage.

"Now I know you're looking at schools with better numbers," Coach said. "But I want you to look at the whole environment. And I believe we're prepared to offer you an environment in which all your needs — not just your needs as an athlete — will be taken care of. Isn't that right, Faith?"

"Absolutely right," I said. Coach tugged on his left earlobe, which was my signal that I was allowed to speak extemporaneously.

"We have excellent academic resources for our student-athletes," I said. "But of course that's after you get here. Whether you choose UT or another Division One school," I said, "there's the question of your eligibility for freshman year."

Coach tugged on his other earlobe, my signal that I was on the wrong track. *No, no!* I could almost hear him thinking. *Don't worry about that! We can fix that somehow!*

The kid stared at his napkin.

"You understand Proposition Sixteen," I said.

"Kid can *run*," his dad said.

"I understand, sir, but if he wants to play for a Division One school next year, he's going to have to either boost his GPA somewhat or hit a higher score on the SAT. Your son scored a combined seven hundred on the SAT, which means he needs a 2.5 GPA to make him eligible. If he could boost his SAT to nine hundred, his current GPA of 2.0 would be acceptable. Every ten-point drop in the SAT score below nine hundred requires a .025 rise in GPA. This is not something I've made up, not something that's in our power to change. It's an NCAA requirement. We're very, very interested in you," I said, and the boy lifted his head and looked me in the eyes. "And if you can make yourself eligible to play for us, I think we can keep you eligible. But you have some work to do right now, a different kind of work from running and catching and lifting weights, and we need to know if you're prepared to do it."

"Let me be honest with you," the boy's father said. "Our boy's Heisman material. The way he runs, he could go all the way. Bring home the hardware. You know what I'm sayin'?"

"Yes, sir," I said. "I sure do."

"And to put up those kinda numbers, he needs the best offensive line he can get, and then even if he *does* put up those kinda numbers, they need to count for something. Kid needs to play for a sure winner. All this mumbo jumbo about SAT scores —"

"Are you looking at some Division Two and Three schools?" I said. "Just in case?" I was suddenly concerned about the boy's future; my own seemed so dark that I wanted to make sure someone's would be okay.

"Now our projections for next year —" Coach started.

"I want some blueberries in my pancakes," the kid said. "I forgot to tell her I want blueberries."

"Faith," Coach said, "go track her down and tell her the kid wants blueberries."

When I got back to the table Coach was reassuring the kid of his all-around worth, academic and otherwise, and before I could sit down he said, "Faith, thanks for joining us, dear, but hadn't you better scoot on to that other meeting?"

"Right," I said. I held out my hand to shake the boy's. "Best of luck to you," I said. "I look forward to seeing you play."

"Thanks," he said.

I knew Coach was angry at me for bringing up the kid's eligibility, but I didn't care. If I had to face the reality that my husband had killed a woman, Coach could certainly face the reality that this blur of speed he was trying to recruit wasn't even eligible to play for us with his current numbers.

I walked out of the restaurant and drove on to the jail, where Jay wore a horrible orange jumpsuit and an aged face. We spoke on a dirty phone and watched each other through scratched Plexiglas. I tried very hard not to let my mouth touch the phone.

"You're looking like quite the teacher this morning," he said.

I wasn't sure what to say back: You're looking like quite the prisoner? Instead I tried to decipher some of the Plexiglas scratchings: "fuk," "R.W. luvs L.M.," and a wavery "No."

"Jay," I said, "what should I do?"

"Always ready to *do* something, aren't you? I'm not a GPA, Faith. You can't fix this one."

"Don't be so obnoxious," I said. "Obviously I can't fix it."

"I fucking killed someone," he said, "in case you hadn't noticed. How can anything be obnoxious compared to that?

You expect these visits to be fun? Romantic? Guess again, teacher."

This was one of my least favorite versions of Jay: bitter, resigned, watching something happen to him as if it were a storm falling from the sky, as if he hadn't engineered the whole damn thing. I realized that the night before, when he had kissed me so sweetly and whispered loving things in my ear, he had still been drunk. Now he was hung over and cruel. I wanted another option.

"Jay," I said, in the patient voice I reserved for my most stubborn athletes, "I'm going to find you a lawyer today and I'll bring him here to meet with you tomorrow morning, okay?"

"Fine," he said. "You're in charge now. Just what you always wanted, right? Perfect way to make me behave, isn't it? Just keep me in a cage."

"In the meantime," I said, my patience gone, "try not to be such an ass."

Then I hung up the phone and walked away.

I'm Glad It Works Somewhere

"Happy Birthday to You" had taken on a twisted significance ever since Jay's pseudogift of a year of sobriety, but nevertheless I sang it with enthusiasm at Micah's combination birthday/going-away party the evening after Jay had been arrested, only hours after my staff and all my student-athletes and everyone else in Austin had heard the terrible news.

Micah was twenty-one years old and had, after his expulsion from UT, been signed by the San Francisco Giants for a perversely large amount of money. Everyone was his buddy again, even Coach Talwen. Everyone was glad we had something to talk about besides my soon-to-be-a-convict husband. No one had said a word to me, but they didn't need to. The hush that had fallen over the room when I walked in had said it all.

"Looks like everything worked out for the best here," Coach said as he sliced the huge cake that read "Good-bye, Mic, We'll Miss You." The cake's message didn't quite capture the facts: We'd already been missing Micah, and Cory, and Mike Winston, enough to lose ten of our last twelve games. I stared at Micah, who wore a gold pinkie ring

LOUISE REDD

shaped like Texas with a diamond representing Austin's location, who had dyed the tip of each of his dreadlocks a metallic blond, who wore a glossy suit, not a shiny suit but a *glossy* suit, and a diamond nose stud and who looked like either a pimp or a rock star, and I thought, *Damn.* I felt strangely cheered. He had been caught with drugs and kicked off the team of which he was the star, he had veered sharply from the course his mother had set for him, and now he was off to live every boy's dream, to play baseball in the major leagues and to get paid millions of dollars to do so. *If only Jay could play a sport,* I thought. *This would probably all be okay.* Too bad drunken frisbee golf didn't have a professional level.

"Got a hot tub in the master bedroom," Micah said, talking about the house he had already bought in California. "All kinds a shit. Got a, what they call it, retractable skylight, and remote control curtains. If I'm layin' in bed I don't have to get up to close the curtains."

The mention of a bed, typically, sent my boys into a frenzy of exchanged sly looks and simmering laughter.

"Micah Levin," I said, "now how are you going to stay in shape if you're too lazy to get up out of bed and close your own curtains?"

"Look at her," he said. "Thinks she's still my teacher. Thinks she can still boss me."

"You just call me if you can't make out all those big words on your contract. I'll help you out for a small fee."

"*Claro,*" Micah said with a perfect Spanish accent.

Then the pitching staff presented Micah with a plaque that said PICK YOUR NOSE with Micah's UT career stats beneath, and Coach blushed while we all laughed and parts of the story that everyone already knew circulated around the room among the laughter.

"— Coach is pissed cause we're on a losing streak, righteously pissed and he gets on one of his wind-sprint kicks, thinks we're fucking basketball players or something —"

"— Mic's run a buttload of sprints and he trips and crashes into this hurdle someone left at the edge of the track, pastes his nose and it's all bleeding and shit —"

"— he's all bent over with his hand over his fucked-up nose, and Coach is up in the stands, but he'd totally missed seeing Mic crash into the thing, and he spots him all bent over down there and he gets his damn bullhorn fired up —"

"— and he yells, 'Christ, Levin! What're ya doin' out there, picking your nose?'"

"What was I supposed to think?" Coach said, his lips growing shiny with spit. "I don't see what's so freakin' funny about that. Probably do the same thing if it happened again."

This sent everybody into a fresh round of laughter, so that most of the boys didn't notice when Cory opened the door to the study lounge and came shuffling in, his torso stiff with bandages. His shirt declared him a member of Team Jesus.

"Bell!" Micah said, standing up and walking toward Cory to exchange an elaborate handshake. Cory hadn't quite met Micah's eyes and I realized he was probably looking around for Mike Winston. I cut a piece of cake for Cory, took it to him, and whispered, "Mike's not here, honey. Everything's okay."

"I've forgiven him, Miss Evers," Cory said.

"Well, sometimes forgiveness doesn't completely do the trick."

"In God's word it does," Cory said.

"I'm glad it works somewhere," I said.

"Miss Evers," Cory whispered, leaning close, "I'm praying for you."

"Thanks, honey," I said, tears suddenly heating my eyes.

It was nice to have the team together again, even though our season was shot, even though it would become progressively more difficult for me to motivate my boys to study when I didn't have the carrot of playoff appearances to dangle in front of them, even though I had heard of a plot among the outfield to intentionally let their grades slip below the qualifying mark so as to escape the last month of our now-pointless season, even though I didn't know what in the world would happen to my marriage. For the moment I ate bite after bite of cake, watched my boys laughing together, and tried to enjoy Micah's predictions of glory and the dreams they set to dancing in all of us.

Mommy's Favorite

"Faith!" Coach Talwen stopped me in the hallway the day after Micah's party, the corners of his mouth bright with saliva. "You're getting a little too popular, it seems."

"What do you mean?" I said, still breathless from a frenzied ten-mile run and, before that, a meeting with Jay and his lawyer at the jail. I leaned against the wall, trying to breathe, trying to locate Coach's eyes in the shade of his baseball cap.

"The cheerleaders want to get in on the tutoring system. I just got out of a meeting with Pam Leland. I know you're overburdened as it is, but if I say no she'll nail me for sexism."

"They're in on the mentoring system already," I said.

"I know, but she wants full-blown support."

"Let's put them in with the women's teams, then."

It would certainly look better if you hadn't hit a woman, the lawyer had said.

"That was my first thought, too. But Pam's beef is that her girls work primarily on the men's schedule and should be given the same quality tutoring as the boys."

How about if he hadn't hit anyone? I'd said in irritation. *That'd probably look fantastic, wouldn't it?*

"There's nothing wrong with the women's tutoring," I said. "I think Janet's done a great job."

"Bottom line is you have the higher passing rate, Faith."

"Well, it's not going to help my boys to give the cheerleaders access to their study areas. We just can't get into that. Give Janet another staff member, I'll help out with the interviewing if you want, and tell Pam we're not running a coed system here and that we need to keep the boys separate to avoid any potential sexual harassment problems."

"Okay, that sounds good. You doing all right? Gonna get through this?"

"Yeah," I said. "I think so." I thought of how grateful I was for my job, of how it might keep me from going crazy, of how happy I was to be part of something. I thought of the orange-and-white banner that hung above the door to the study lounge: TEAM: TOGETHER EVERYONE ACHIEVES MORE. "Look," I said, "if you want me to meet with Pam, I'll be glad to tell her myself." And I meant it; everything seemed easy compared with being married to a man who'd committed vehicular manslaughter.

"I might take you up on that," Coach said.

"Or I can not be there and you can just blame everything on me."

I'm sorry I was such a jerk yesterday, Jay had said. *I'm sorry I've been such a jerk for such a long time. If you want to take back your promise . . .*

My promise to you still stands, I'd said. *My promise to you is etched in stone, okay?*

"Either way," Coach said. "I'll let you know. You hang in there, Faith."

"I will," I said.

Coach wandered down the hall and I wandered toward the study room where some of the pitchers were playing cards. "You guys are supposed to be reading Juan Rulfo," I said. "I distinctly heard the T.A. warn you to be ready for a pop quiz tomorrow. Go on, now, go get your books and come right back."

"After this hand," said Joey Glenn.

I snatched the cards from his fist, tossed them down on the table, and said, "Now. Go on. You'll like the story. It's all about a girl's breasts."

"No shit?" Andy said. He threw down his cards and said, "Come on."

"You don't have to be such a bitch," Joey said, pulling on the lid of his cap.

"And you don't have to make a crappy grade in this class," I said. "And if you ever call me a bitch again you're going to be out of my program, Joey. Coach will stand behind me on that." *Only because you're a rotten pitcher*, I could have added. I also could have added that Joey failed exams for the same reason he failed in games: short attention span. He was masterful through four innings, and could write about half of a decent essay, but was incapable of completing anything. I figured he'd end up a middle reliever, though I nursed a secret hope that he'd mature into a starter.

"Come on," Andy said, "let's get our books, man. She doesn't need this shit right now."

Joey stood up but couldn't keep from muttering something about how it's not his fault *your husband's a fucking drunk* and I decided, with every bit of willpower I could scrape up, to ignore him.

All four of them shuffled off to get their books. I sat down and waited for them and thought about what kind of job I might get that didn't involve any bossing around: performance artist, playing some little stringed instrument with toothpicks?

But we got through the evening, didn't we, we managed to analyze a story in which a young girl's breasts are discussed often and in detail with a minimum of giggles and pokes and hyperactive eyebrows. And Joey said, his cap turned backward so I could see the swimming-pool blue of his eyes, "Sorry I called you that, Miss Evers."

"It's okay," I said. "I'm sorry I have to nag you so much but it's my job."

"Yeah, I know," he said.

Grow, grow, grow, Mother would nag her tomatoes while the child version of me trailed her through the garden. *You there, now, stop crowding your neighbor. And you, you should be a little sturdier with all the goodies I've given you. Oh, here's my baby. Look, Faith, this one is Mommy's favorite.*

Throughout the past two days, my parents and Darrah and half my staff and even my aunt Ruth had left frantic messages on my answering machine, demanding to know *What on earth, what the fuck, Jesus, Faith, is this true?* I had put off calling anyone back, but finally I couldn't delay any longer, and when I went back to my room that night, I picked up the phone and began to dial.

A Whole New Ball Game

What happened to me over the next week was not what people expected: the shifts in my heart, the final settling, the certainty of my feeling that I loved Jay, that I wanted to try to love him through this thing and beyond it. Not that love is enough. Even then, I wasn't so foolish as to think love would be enough.

Daddy said, "Well, honey, it's a good thing you'd already taken some steps toward getting away. Do you want to talk to your mother?"

"No," I said.

Coach Talwen said, "You're still young, Faith. You can still have a life, remarry, have children."

Darrah said, "Knowing Jay, I'm surprised it wasn't an entire school bus full of handicapped Christian orphans or something. Please tell me you're divorcing him."

From county jail, where Jay still wore an orange jumpsuit so hideous it made my Texas Longhorns gear look almost attractive, he told me, "Buddy, I know you said you'd wait for me, and I'm not doubting you at all, your ability to do that, but maybe you've wasted enough time on me. You're young and smart and gorgeous and I don't want you to blow another minute of your life on my drunk ass, if you don't want to. You heard what the lawyer said; it could be five years, and that's if I'm lucky. If you want to get the divorce papers cooking, I'll sign them, Faith. You won't ever have to look back." He looked down as he said it. He was afraid to even look at me, afraid he might see me nodding in agreement.

"Shut up, Jay," I said. "I'm waiting for you and I'm expecting you to come out of jail a completely sober and changed person, and it's up to you to live up to that. I don't care if it's ten years. We both have a job ahead of us so let's just try to do it, okay?"

"Okay," he said. "Okay."

It was after that visit to the jail, on a Tuesday afternoon, that I decided to go to a baseball game. I wanted to go for a run, but I was afraid if I started running, I might never stop. I was afraid of where I'd end up. So instead I walked over to the field, where my boys were playing LSU, and found a seat along the first-base line. It was a gorgeous day; most of the people around me looked as if they were there more for the sunbathing opportunities than for the baseball. My boys were winning 1–0.

I hardly recognized the team without Mike Winston at short, without Micah on the mound, without Cory at second base. Billy Reed, a freshman out of El Paso, had been moved into the rotation to fill Micah's spot; he was slowly getting hammered. Or maybe it would be more accurate to say he was hammering himself, getting ahead in the count and then letting it run full, throwing a couple of perfect fastballs in a row and then switching over to his weaker, wilder breaking ball. When I sat down, Billy had runners on first and second; he walked the next batter to load the bases. The LSU fans on the other side of the field began to perk up as they realized that Billy was handing them a whole new ball game. Billy threw two searing fastballs for strikes but followed them with a pitch in the dirt that was just barely recovered by Pete, the catcher, in time to keep the runner on third from coming home. I didn't know Pete too well — he was smart and stayed on top of his classes and very rarely needed my help — but I thought he was a decent catcher.

Someone behind me said, "This guy sucks."

Then, as if to confirm it, Billy threw two more balls; one more would mean he'd walk a run home. I couldn't see Coach from where I was sitting, but I could imagine his face: creased and red in patches, marbled like a hunk of meat. I imagined he was spitting at a faster-than-normal rate. Billy took a long time adjusting his cap. Pete ran out to talk to him; the count stalled at 3–2. But finally, Billy couldn't put it off any longer, and he threw the pitch that became ball four and gave LSU a free run. Coach came barreling out of the dugout. Billy hung his head, tugged on the bill of his cap, dug the toe of his sneaker in the dirt.

I leaned back, looked up at the hot blue sky, and smiled. It was a beautiful thing, to watch someone failing so horribly in a way that didn't even matter, to see someone failing in a *game*. It was nice to sit back in the bleachers on a sunny afternoon, on a big, rich, university campus, to know that every one of those boys could fall flat on his face out there, that Billy could walk the entire opposing team home, and it still wouldn't matter. They would all go on and grow up a little more and find wives and breed little babies and wait for those babies to grow big enough to play catch, to catch a baseball in their darling little hands. They would buy houses, shore up the foundations and repair faulty wiring, plant trees in the yards and position sprinklers to help usher those trees through our long, long summers. While they did all this, Jay would be in prison, Alice Jamison would be dead; and me? I would continue getting up and going to work and eating and sleeping and trying to keep my love for my husband fresh in my heart. I would slog through day after day with the assumption that things would be better soon. It was a belief so contrary to all available evidence that you'd almost have to call it faith.

PART II

"It's what you learn after
you know it all that counts."

— *Earl Weaver*

Brandywine

When your husband has recently killed a beautiful young woman, a young social worker full of potential, a young woman whose picture on the front page of the paper is underscored with captions like "Worked with the poor in her spare time" and "Had dreams of building a shelter for abused children," this is what will happen:

Angry, threatening letters, vitriolic letters, will crowd your mailbox. A typical letter will say: "Your husband should fry for what he did to that sweet young woman. He killed her as surely as if he had stuck a gun to her head. How does it feel to be married to a murderer?" Other letters will arrive from treatment centers, lawyers, Mothers Against Drunk Driving. Some will contain photographs of victims of drunk drivers, glowing little children and teenagers with a grit of acne on their chins and braces crowding their mouths. In with the piles of letters will be bills you're not sure how you will pay, now that your husband, the drunken murderer, has lost his job and will be in jail for who knows how long.

Your relatives, down to vaguely remembered cousins and

with the exception of your mother, will leave mostly encouraging messages on your answering machine, messages like "We're thinking of you, honey," and this from your aunt Meryl in New York: "My dear, here in the city that's what we call a 'starter marriage.' Just move right along, precious. Just move right along and don't look back."

Your best friend will bring you slabs of chocolate, trays of brownies. She will come to your dorm room on a very bad night and give you a facial, for which you will love her forever and ever. Through the slit of your mouth, the mud pack drying around it, you will tell her you're tired of being the nonaddicted one, that you want to take up smoking or something. You will try to convince her to go out with you to buy a pack of cigarettes and smoke them all. "I can't," she will say, her fingers light on your forehead. "I'm nursing. My body is a temple." In spite of the chocolate and the facials and your certainty that she *would* help you cultivate some addiction if her body were not at this moment a temple, you will suffer bouts of worry that she has stopped trying to teach her child how to say "Aunt Faith" and especially "Uncle Jay."

You will endure horrible embarrassment because now everybody knows the secret you had worked so hard to keep. You will feel like a hypocrite in front of your athletes, in front of the boys to whom you've repeatedly said things like "Good character builds a good team," because now there is no hiding the fact that your own personal team, the team of Faith and Jay, is a big, fat loser. You will be grateful that it's summer school, that your boys are busy taking GPA-inflating classes like Music of the 1970's and In-Line Skating for Everyone and Golf Course Design for Beginners, classes for which they rarely need your help. Cory Bell, who is excelling in Oaxacan Ceramics, will come to you and say, "Miss Evers, are you ready yet?," meaning are you ready, in your weakened state, to let Jesus Christ weasel His way into your life. You will barely refrain from telling Cory that if there is a God, you are ready to stab His or Her eyeballs out with a dull, rusty fork. "No, honey," you will say, and because he is so disappointed you will add, "maybe soon, sweetheart."

Your husband's drunken extravaganza will, horribly, coincide with National Drunk Driving Awareness Month. A group of activists will cover the lawn of the Capitol in empty pairs of shoes, one pair for each person killed that year by a drunk driver. You will force yourself to go to the Capitol to look at the gaping shoes: high heels, work boots, sneakers half the size of your hand. You will fight the urge to kick off your own black clogs and run away across the shimmering-hot parking lot, screaming and barefoot.

You will wake in the middle of the night and lace on your running shoes and run mile after mile through the campus, through the city, through neighborhoods where you could be hurt or killed. Potential criminals will be made lazy by your speed, by the determined slap of your shoes; they will wait for someone more slovenly, less fierce, to pass by.

After a while, your boss will ask, tactfully, if you might need some time off. He will phrase it as if it's to your advantage, as if the time off will help you gather your thoughts, pull yourself together, make a plan for the future. You won't tell him that time off would only give your thoughts the chance to eat you alive, that time off might allow you the space to realize how awful things really are. You won't tell him you're afraid that time off is just a euphemism for "you're fired." You will work harder than ever. You will have the math tutor help you design a chart that plots the improvement in the athletes' grades during your time as head tutor. You will keep this chart under your bed, in case it's needed, in case someone thinks you haven't been doing a good job.

You will start going to church, even though you have never gone to church, even though you spent every Sunday morning of your childhood helping your mother weed her garden. In your mind, this church has nothing to do with the Jesus of Cory's T-shirts but is a place where you can sit quietly, where no one will call you Miss Evers or ask for your help. You will sit in the back row of the multidenominational service in the campus chapel and hurl prayers out into the void, vague prayers that would never survive the rigors of a basic composition course, that would, if they appeared in one of your students' essays, cause you to demand that the writer *be more specific*.

You will sell the house in which you once thought you'd grow old with the man you love, the drunk murderer husband. You will make a profit, because Austin is booming, because it's a seller's market, and you will stare out the car window while your realtor, whose cell phone is so often next to her head that you start to think of it as a big, clunky earring, chatters about the fabulous market, about how lucky you are. The week before the closing, you will hire two second-string basketball players to stack your beautiful furniture in a U-Haul and you will drive it to Houston, where your parents have agreed to store it for you in two of their many unused rooms. You will not see your mother on this dumping-the-furniture trip; she will be in Dallas giving a speech about her giant tomato, a speech your father tells you is titled "The Big One."

You will wear your wedding ring again, desperate for physical proof that your husband exists.

When the station manager calls to tell you to come get the rest of Jay's things, the CDs and interview notes and fish-shape cat treats, he will say, "Faith, this is the worst thing that could possibly have happened for the station. The negative publicity could *kill* us. Of course, I mean obviously, we'll have to let him go."

"Speak for yourself," you tell him, and he doesn't understand what you mean.

On returning from the station with Jay's things, you feed the cat so many fish-shape treats that he becomes ill all over Joey Glenn's essay about *Hamlet,* your favorite line of which is "Hamlet's mother was something of a slut."

Near the end of summer school, you will ask your father to take the cat, because a dorm in fall is no place for a cat; you fear what the new athletes, the ones who don't yet know and depend on you, might do to the animal. This is not the ideal time to ask a favor of your parents. Your mother's mood is reportedly foul because her giant tomato did not break the world record; the day she picked it, the day it was supposed to be weighed on national television, it sprung a leak and collapsed under its own luscious weight. Your father, the doctor, has suggested that she is in a state of mild shock. From her shocked and shaken state, your father tells you, she has reluctantly agreed to take the cat, but refuses to call him Grace, his name. She will rename him Brandywine, after her favorite type of tomato. She will claim, as many people do, that cats don't recognize their names anyway, that they don't know what the hell you're talking about. You will hire the second-string nose guard, who is trapped in summer school, to drive to Houston with you and carry the cat up to your parents' door so you will not have to see your mother.

"Your mom's cute," the nose guard says on returning to the car.

"Shut up," you say, perversely glad he is the only person in the history of the university to be failing Golf Course Design for Beginners. Giving up the cat, and the cat's real name, will for some reason let loose a flood of sorrow that's been barely under control all summer. Driving away from Grace/Brandywine and Houston, you will cry, right in front of the nose guard, the tears you held back each time the lawyer called to regale you with some lawyerly nonsense, the tears you didn't cry when he told you your husband had decided to plead guilty to one count of vehicular manslaughter, the tears you didn't cry each time you changed the word in your mind to *womanslaughter*.

If you wait long enough, people will stop asking. They will begin to pretend that you don't *have* a husband. They will, in conversation, focus mostly on your job, on how interesting it is, how satisfying it must be. Your girlfriends' husbands will talk sports to you as if you are a coach instead of a tutor, as if you have some control over the outcome of a game. They will treat you as if you are single, mentioning supposedly interesting single men from work, inviting you to parties which include these supposedly interesting single men, never turning the radio to Jay's former station in your presence. You will follow their example, most of the time, except on the days when you have a little something extra, enough spare strength to remember what it was like to sleep in the arms of a man you loved, what it might be like to do so again.

My Husband Works Hard at His Dental Clinic

Because Jay had never before been arrested, never convicted of a felony or even a misdemeanor, and perhaps because he was a nice-looking white boy, our lawyer was able to wrangle for him a choice in exchange for his guilty plea: either a four-year prison sentence or two and a half years in the Perryton-Henley unit of the Texas department of corrections, where they would supposedly teach him all sorts of skills for staying sober. The lawyer warned us that the Perryton-Henley choice would not be as easy as prison, that some people chose the longer sentence rather than face the work of becoming sober. "In prison you have no worries," he told us. "You just kick back and watch TV. In there you'll have people in your face all the time, calling you on your issues." Jay said he'd never been much of a TV watcher anyway, and the lawyer laughed.

I felt tempted to answer my hate mail from the people who wrote me in protest of Jay's light sentence, like the one from a person who sent a clipping about a man in Colorado who received a fifteen-year sentence for illegally killing cougars. "Apparently the life of a Texas woman is worth less than the life of a Colorado cougar," this person wrote in bleedy letters in the margin of the newspaper.

I never answered the letters because I didn't know what to say. I knew only that each day felt like a year, that I lived and died by the speed of the mail between the Perryton-Henley unit in Dayton, Texas, forty miles east of Houston, and Austin. My disappointment on the days when my mailbox was empty was so sharp that I contrived ways of always having *something* in there. I subscribed to magazines that had never before interested me. I sent away for catalogs full of things I didn't need: gardening supplies, kitchen gadgets, lingerie. On Saturdays, when I drove to Dayton for my weekly visit with Jay, I mailed myself postcards that promised me everything would be all right, that encouraged me to be patient and strong. When encouraging words refused to exit my pen, I filled the postcards with bits of favorite poems: "I staggered banged with terror through a million billion trillion stars," or "Those friends thou hast, and their adoption tried/Grapple them to thy soul with hoops of steel . . ."

I cried all the time, mostly for Alice Jamison, but sometimes from relief that Jay's drinking life was finally over, sometimes from the sharpness of missing him, from not knowing what our marriage would be like without the drinking and without my nagging about it, without anything as we had known it.

I ran mile after mile, until my tendons ached, until my heels were bruised. Sometimes while I ran I tried thinking up an answer to the question the Mistress had asked me, about why I was attracted to such a person as Jay. I ran faster and faster, but no answer came to my mind.

I answered an ad on the English department bulletin

board for a third-grade class in Oklahoma that needed pen pals, and their teacher assigned me to an eight-year-old girl named Tonía. Tonía wrote to me, in half print, half cursive, about her brothers and sisters, her above-ground swimming pool, her hamster and the frightening noises it made at night. I filled her mailbox with extravagant lies about my marriage to a dentist, my three lovely daughters, and the big house we all lived in. I wrote about the tree house my husband had built for our daughters, in the large live oak in our backyard, how he had placed a trampoline under the tree house in case one of our precious girls should fall out of it. When Tonía wrote back and asked to know the names of my girls, I had a wonderful time naming them: Ellen Anne was my oldest child, my smart, quiet child who was never without a book. Emily was my middle daughter, who loved to play soccer and cruise the Internet, under my supervision of course. And Claire was my baby, just a year old, named after my mother. "My husband works hard at his dental clinic," I wrote, "and he talks quite a bit about the teeth of people I've never met. This can get boring sometimes, but I love him very much."

Jay's letters varied wildly in tone: Some were sexual, some abject, some angry and bored. Sometimes he thanked me profusely for sticking with him, for agreeing to wait for him to serve his time. Other times he ordered me to forget about him, to go out and find someone new and to forget about his lousy, fucked-up, jailbird self.

"Dear Buddy," he wrote.

I'm deep into the treatment part of my day at the moment. We are currently playing the quiet game, as we have been for the last twenty-two minutes. Oh, boy! Only eight minutes to go. Before that we played hangman for an hour, using alternative phrases to "no," the idea being that we will use these helpful phrases once we get the heck out of here and someone offers us drugs or booze. The scintillating game of hangman, plus the quiet time, counts as an hour and a half of the twenty hours a week of treatment this company is required to give us per their contract with the State of Texas. I'm practically cured already, can't you tell? Just kidding. On an agonizingly truthful note, I miss every inch of your body and face. I must have been a saint in a former life, because I obviously haven't done anything in this one to deserve a wife like you.

At the end of that letter was a postscript asking me to please place the enclosed letter on Alice Jamison's grave. I understood then that he had been writing about hangman and quiet time in order to avoid saying what he really wanted to say: Here's a letter written to a dead woman, a woman who is dead because of me.

It took me a few days to find out where she was buried, and then a few more to get up the courage to go to her grave, but I finally did it one Thursday around lunchtime, in between Intermediate French and a meeting with the cheerleaders' coach. I had a hard time deciding what to wear; it seemed disrespectful to wear my usual jeans and longhorn-plastered T-shirt, but I wasn't going to a funeral, after all. Finally I settled on a black cotton sundress and black sandals.

At the cemetery in North Austin I realized it might take me hours to find Alice Jamison's grave; rows of flat, uniform markers stretched in every direction. I walked two rows, looking at the name on each plaque, before a man on a riding lawn mower drove by and I waved him down. He seemed glad for a chance to stop the noise of the mower. He wiped his wet face with a red towel and said, "What can I do ya for?"

"I'm trying to find someone's grave and I have no idea where it is."

As he pointed toward the maintenance shack in one corner of the cemetery, as he told me about the laminated chart I'd find tacked to the outside wall, I couldn't help thinking one of my mother's thoughts: that he shouldn't be mowing in the middle of the day, that cutting the grass at high noon subjected it to unnecessary stress.

"Thank you so much," I said, and he said, "What did the blonde say to the turtle?"

"Please don't," I said, and I walked quickly away.

The mower's engine didn't start up again until I was almost halfway across the cemetery, heading toward the shack. The chart showed Alice Jamison's location as E-4, which turned out to be a section along the chain-link fence on the east side of the cemetery. I sat down in the warm grass by her marker and tried to ignore the sound of the cars rushing by. I thought it must be nice at night, when the traffic quieted.

I set Jay's letter on the marker in between two bouquets of dried yellow roses and found a small rock to hold it there. Alice Jamison had been born the same year as Jay, two months before him. They had come into the world at roughly the same time, had learned to hold a fork and to do their multiplication tables and to say "yes, ma'am" and "no, sir," had heard the same songs on the radio and had watched the same presidents on television, had gulped their first drinks without knowing that one of them was meeting a demon while the other was simply having her first drink, without knowing that after all that parallel growing, one would take the life of the other.

"Excuse me," a voice said from behind me. I stood up quickly, brushed the grass from the back of my dress. I saw a young man holding a cluster of yellow roses, the short-stemmed fragrant kind that don't last long once they're cut. "I'm Richard Jamison," he said. "Her husband. And you are?"

"Faith Evers," I said, feeling sick in the pit of my heart but holding out my hand anyway. I looked over my shoulder, as if Alice's mother, her grandmother, her first-grade teacher, and everyone else who ever loved her might suddenly be converging on me. After a terrible moment I realized that he wasn't going to extend his hand, so I took mine back.

"The drunk's wife," he said, hands stiffly around the roses.

"Yes."

"Well, Faith Evers," he said. "Are you done soothing your guilt or whatever the hell it is you're here to do? Because I'd like to spend some time with my wife."

Despite his curt, hostile tone, he looked like a tired little boy. He wore an Allman Brothers T-shirt with a giant peach on the front. He wore cut-off shorts and sneakers with no socks. His hair was the stiff, chlorinated blond of a child who's spent too much time in the swimming pool. He looked like he should have been home napping in a hammock, or tinkering with his lawn mower, instead of bringing roses to a grave.

"I'm sorry," I said. "My husband asked me to bring this letter out here, so I did. I didn't mean to intrude."

He bent down and snatched the letter from underneath the rock. He unfolded it and started to read it, then crumpled it into a ball and hurled it over the chain-link fence, into the passing traffic. I recognized in his eyes a dry redness that comes when you've cried about all the tears your body can stand to cry, when your eyes simply can't manufacture another drop of moisture. I had the sensation that he might hit me, and if he had, I don't think I would have screamed or run away. I think I would have stood there and let him, hoping it would help one or the other of us. But instead he stared at the roses in his left hand as if they were the source of his problems, as if they were the ugliest things he had ever seen. I started to edge away, the metal of the fence hot against my back. He ran a hand through his straight blond hair, his hand curling into a fist against his scalp.

"Are you staying married to him?" he said, still looking at the flowers. Then, "I'm sorry. It's none of my business."

"I'm staying with him," I said. "But not because I think what he did is okay."

He hummed a little bit of "Stand By Your Man," a horrible, wavering, operatic humming. He looked crazed; I wouldn't have been surprised if he had stuffed those roses in his mouth and chewed them into a pudding. I kept moving away, step by tiny step.

"Would you maybe talk to me sometime?" he called, when I was already six or seven graves away from Alice's. I turned and looked at him. "People are sick of hearing me talk about it," he said. "And I know you've lost something too."

I nodded, because what he'd said had closed up my throat and choked off my voice too much to speak. Then I pulled one of my business cards from my purse, walked back to Alice's grave, and handed it to him, and we both smiled a little, the small, weak sort of smile that comes when things are so bad that you might as well smile, when there's nothing left to do *but* smile.

Imagine Something Long

Sometimes I understood what Gisela was talking about and sometimes I just let her commanding voice jolt by me as I twisted myself into some yoga pose, some pose that I hoped would bring so much blood to my brain that there would be no room for confusion. "When we do *this*," Gisela said, cranking her neck into an example of what we should not do, "we do not *focus* our energy but we *fling* it all over the place in a rather *messy* way." I loved the way she said *fling*; she said it as if she were tossing handfuls of confetti into a great, violent wind. Gisela's specialty, besides speaking in such an entertaining manner, was demonstrating what we should *not* do, making a sad lump of her back, a horrible protrusion of her lumbar spine, a compressed accordion of her neck. I saw myself in her in these moments, when she purposefully wrung her straight, perfect body into something awful, and I felt relieved when she once again lengthened her neck, when she restored the integrity of her spine. I realized, as I strained to complete the triangle pose without scrunching my neck into my shoulders, why Jay's book of hangover cures annoyed me so much, why it made me think of Gisela in one of her intentionally distorted poses: because I didn't see the beauty in a cure for a self-inflicted injury, because the whole thing reminded me too much of my marriage.

"*Lengthen,* Faith," Gisela said. "Show me how *long* your neck can be." From deep within my collapsed triangle, I lengthened a bit. "Imagine something *long,*" Gisela said. "Maybe it is a long, long road. Maybe it is the distance between you and another person. Perhaps it is a stretch of beach you once walked along. Or maybe it is the distance between today and your next vacation." Someone on the other side of the room laughed, a short, harsh laugh with a raw, jagged ending. "Imagine this long thing and then make your neck as long as that," Gisela said. *"Ask* it to be as long as the thing you have in your mind."

I had so many long things in my life it was impossible to choose: the distance between Austin and Dayton, Texas; the stretch of time until I would see Jay; the uncrossable difference between Darrah's life and mine, Darrah with her happy marriage and her beautiful baby, the baby with such luxurious rolls of fat that Darrah had to pry them open to let water in when she bathed the child, each roll of fat signifying some richness in Darrah's life; the miles that could be covered by taking every dollar bill Jay had spent on marijuana, beer, and gin and setting them end on end, the number of times that rope of money could wrap around our little world. I finally settled on the length of one of Mother's rows of tomatoes, and when I closed my eyes I could see it perfectly: Mother ahead of me saying, "Look at this one, Faith," her back to me but no doubt in my mind that she was smiling. I stretched my neck to get closer to her; I lengthened until I could almost touch her. I wanted to be friends with my mother, lovers with my husband. I wanted to figure out the answer to the question the Mistress had asked me. I wanted Jay and me to be winners in the Game of Life.

"Good, Faith," Gisela said. "That's looking *quite* good. I can tell that you have a nice, long thing in your mind."

I stretched my neck even longer, impossibly long, willing to stay in the triangle pose forever if that's what it took for someone to tell me I was good.

Aunt Faith and Uncle Jay

Sometimes I turned on the radio expecting to hear Jay's voice encouraging some loser to expound on a chicken soup with beer recipe. Instead I heard a stranger speaking, or music Jay never would have played. I clicked off the radio in shock, as if I were hanging up from an obscene phone call.

The radio wasn't the only thing that routinely shocked me; throughout the end of that scalding hot summer and the start of the warm fall that followed it, Richard Jamison and I became friends. I was occupied with football season, my busiest time of the year, but about once a week we'd meet at Las Manitas and eat too many quesadillas and talk. We talked a lot about Alice, about the person she'd been; one day Richard told me how she'd loved Woody Allen's films and had continued loving them in spite of his personal humiliations.

"Alice said that if she knew everything about the personal lives of all the artists and writers she admired, she'd probably find out things far worse than what came out about Woody. She was adamant about not letting anything infringe on her admiration of his work."

"Well, Dostoyevsky supposedly pawned his wife's coat in

the middle of winter so he could gamble, but that doesn't change anything about the quality of his novels for me. Everyone's a jerk when you really get down to it."

"You're not," he said. He ate chips and salsa the same way I did, scooping salsa onto the chip instead of the weaker method of dipping the chip in and out to achieve a thin coating of salsa.

"I am," I said. "You just don't know me well enough."

"Tell me one jerky thing you've done," he said. "Besides marry a drunk." He set down his water glass with a sound like a gavel. I waited one, two, three beats before he said, "Sorry. I'm crazy. You should know that I'm crazy. So, let's hear it. Tell me something horrible about yourself."

"I can't," I said. "First of all, the list is too long. We'd have to stay here through dinner. And second, you wouldn't like me anymore. I have to keep this illusion that I'm a nice person going as long as possible, or I won't have anyone to listen to me whine."

"I'd listen to you anyway," he said, the meanness in his eyes gone.

"What about you? Are you hiding a jerk somewhere in there?"

"God, Faith, I just . . . sometimes I think about fights Alice and I had and I just cringe. I wish I could take back every rude word I ever said to her. I think about times I made her cry and it just kills me, and then I have to go out in the alley and break stuff. I've broken so many dishes I've started buying paper plates. That's pretty pathetic, isn't it? Alice would strangle me if she knew I've busted all our china. But she had so little time here and I made her cry during some of it, you know? That calls for breaking things."

"Yeah, I know."

"It makes me sick."

"I know. Do you ever run?"

"Only when someone's chasing me."

"It helps."

"Nothing helps, Faith."

We went on like that until we were too sick to eat any more, until Richard, who was a Web designer, said he was glad he had a job where he didn't have to deal with people face to face, where he could just sit at the computer and cry. Then we both went back to work, and I did the deep, even breathing that helps me not cry, and I don't know what he did.

Later that night, I drove up to Darrah's to babysit for a teething Lucy. Darrah had warned me that she might scream all night, but I didn't even care. I was just happy for an excuse to get out of my dorm room, to be heading toward my friend's house, speeding up Lamar past stores where Jay and I used to shop, past the park where Jay used to spend his Saturdays playing drunken games of frisbee golf with his drunken friends. I saw a group of boys, shirts off and tucked into the back pockets of their shorts, baseball caps turned backward, dragging a cooler on wheels through the last, warm light of the evening. The Jay I had known would have thought a cooler with wheels was a wonderful thing; he would have talked for a good long while about the possibilities. I wondered what he thought of as wonderful now. I wondered what kinds of things had filled in the parts of his brain that loved beer and marijuana and four-foot bongs and specialized coolers.

When I arrived, Danny was waiting on the porch, and I could hear Lucy crying inside.

"Taking a break?" I said. He lifted his head from where it had been resting in his hands.

"Hey, Faith," he said, standing up to kiss my cheek. "How are you?"

"Great," I said. "I mean, okay. Sorry. I'm used to faking it."

"How's the team?"

"No one's failing anything and no one's been arrested yet."

"Banner year, huh?"

"Yeah."

He looked at his watch.

"Reservations?"

"Yeah, eight o'clock. Dar hasn't been able to get her calmed down."

"Leave it to Aunt Faith," I said, and he wished me luck as I walked inside.

As Darrah transferred the screeching baby from her hip to mine, she shouted that Lucy would probably do better if I walked her around the house, that she seemed to like that better than holding still. She yelled out some other instructions too, and I nodded, but they got lost in the din of Lucy's screams and my surprise over Darrah's short hair. She'd cut it elfin-short when Lucy was about four months old and starting to grab at everything, but it still surprised me every time. I shouted back that everything would be fine, to go on and have a nice grown-up dinner. She practically ran out of the house, and Lucy and I started walking.

After two or three circles around the house, kitchen to living room to office to bedroom to extra bedroom, her screams turned to sobs and then to little whimpers and then she quieted altogether and involved herself in tugging fiercely on my hair. It hurt, but not as much as the screeching.

"Feel better, baby girl?" I said. I saw the gleam of two tiny, intruding teeth before she stuffed her mouth with my hair. Heat steamed off her face. We walked some more, and I thought how messy Darrah and Daniel's house had been ever since Lucy's birth, how I liked it so much better. The fridge, which had once been covered with newspaper articles and pamphlets about things that outraged Darrah — overpopulation, health care issues — was now crammed with brightly colored magnetic letters of the alphabet. I rearranged the letters to spell out AUNT FAITH LOVES UNCLE JAY. The real question, though, the one I didn't address with Lucy's magnetized alphabet, was whether Uncle Jay would ever love Aunt Faith more than he loved his bottles of gin, his cases of beer, his marijuana Fed Exed from Oregon that was so potent he called it "wheelchair weed." If I could have spelled out the answer to that question with Lucy's bright, smooth letters, I might have known what the future held for us. But I didn't have an answer, so instead I started talking about Jay, to convince myself that he was real, that he was a real person who might someday love me the way I wanted to be loved.

"Do you remember Uncle Jay?" I asked Lucy. "He loves mangoes," I said as she gave my hair a particularly ferocious tug. "Okay, I'm walking," I said. "Look, we're going into Mommy and Daddy's room. Now listen to Aunt Faith's story about the mangoes. We'd eat them all summer — grilled, in salsa, in smoothies, and just plain, of course. Jay spent a semester of college in Kenya, first hiking across the desert and then hanging out on the coast. Said he smoked the most incredible weed there, that everyone smoked it, even old ladies and little children. Jay was in heaven, I'm sure. But anyway, he said the first day he got to the coast, this old guy got him really stoned and gave him a mango, and Jay waded out into the water, until he was pretty far out but still standing, and then he peeled that mango and stood there in the salt water eating it. He said it was one of the best moments of his life — standing in this beautiful salt water eating a mango. What do you think about that, sweet baby? You'd probably like mango, if we mushed it up for you a little. Your little half teeth could probably handle that. What else about your uncle Jay? Sometimes we're afraid we'll forget him, aren't we? Sometimes we're afraid he'll get out of jail and we won't know who in the world he is.

"He wears boxers. I like that.

"When he's drunk he listens to blues, but when he's sober he listens to jazz.

"He writes great letters, and he has beautiful handwriting.

"When I first took Jay home to meet my mother, she said right away, 'Jay, I want to show you our tree.' Then she took him to the back of the yard where there's a massive live oak — she says it's over two hundred years old — and my mother and Jay patted its trunk and looked up in it and I thought about all the boys I'd brought home and how Jay was the only one she'd wanted to take out to our tree. That's how I knew he was the one for me, Luce. Daddy didn't walk out to the tree with us, but you know what he said about Jay? 'He's a keeper,' he said, talking about Jay as if he were a fish."

"Ayyyyauuuuuh," Lucy said.

Darrah had told me to imitate any sound Lucy made, that this would build her self-esteem and encourage her linguistic development, but I couldn't bring myself to do it. Instead I said, "Oh yeah? Well same to you, cutie. Now listen to Aunt Faith. Jay had this big American flag hanging in his room, in the place he lived our junior year. One night we'd made love, which is something fun you'll find out about when you're older, and then we wanted to go out to the kitchen to get some food, but we didn't know if the roommates were around or not, and Jay took the flag down and wrapped me in it and he put on some boxers and we went to the kitchen and made nachos. I remember the flag was very cold against my skin; it was some kind of really synthetic, weatherproof material, I guess — and it was a warm night, almost summer — and it felt so good to be sitting in Jay's kitchen wrapped up in that cool flag.

"Oh, here's a good one. After our wedding, when we were riding from the church to the reception, Jay turned to me and smiled and said, 'Faith, I think I married better than you did.' I remember thinking, *Are you kidding?* Here, let's look in the mirror. See the baby? She just happens to be the most gorgeous baby ever born. See the amazing baby? Someday your uncle Jay and I will have a baby, I swear we will. We'll have a baby and she'll never know her daddy used to drink. She won't know a thing about it. We're just letting her skip this yucky part, aren't we?

"I remember the first time I got mad at Jay about his drinking. We were in a restaurant, and I felt kind of sick, and we were at the end of our meal anyway; they'd taken our plates away and Jay was drinking a beer. I told Jay I felt

weird, that I wanted to get out of there, and when the waitress came he said, 'Could I get one more of these and the
check?' I was so mad that he'd ordered another beer with the
check. He wasn't even finished with the one he was drinking, and he'd had God only knows how many before that,
and here I'd just told him I wanted to leave and he had to get
another beer. I said something to him, and he thought I was
being ridiculous, and that was sort of the start of it. After
that I always felt like his drinking came first, that I was just
along for the ride. But that's all over, Lucy. Every day it's a
little closer to being over."

I talked to Lucy about Jay because I feared forgetting him.
I feared the day when I wouldn't be able to call up Jay's
voice, when I wouldn't be able to close my eyes and see his
face, when even the bad memories would have faded to
nothing, when I'd look back at the version of myself that
loved Jay and think, *Who was* she?

She was a woman who stood up in a simple white silk
dress and swore vow after vow to Jason Markson Evers
without ever thinking the words *in drunkenness and sobriety,
I thee wed.*

She was a woman whose husband didn't have a drinking
problem; he just hadn't yet made the transition from college
to real life, he had an intense job from which he needed to
unwind, and unwind, and unwind, he was just having a
good time with his friends, he was so *sociable*, such a people
person, and beer doesn't have nearly the alcohol content that
liquor does, he just really liked the *taste* of beer, he was a
beer *connoisseur*, and beer is really just liquid bread anyway,
beer is food, you know. And gin, well . . . it's a nice warm-

weather drink, never mind that the weather is almost always warm in Texas.

She was a woman who wanted to be loved the way her mother's garden was loved: constantly, powerfully, with deepest respect.

And another thing: Jay was a creative person, and a lot of creative people have relied on alcohol either to get them cranked up or to bring them down. Jay came up with a lot of his best ideas for his show when he was high and/or drunk, and who was she to take that away from him?

She was a woman who'd thought if she filled her husband's life with love, if she crammed love into every desolate corner, there wouldn't be any room for booze.

And then there's the Texas thing. People in Texas just *drink*.

She was a woman who'd made the mistake of thinking a wedding actually has something to do with a marriage, that it sets the tone somehow, that it's a forecast of things to come. She'd had a hell of a wedding, with the reception in the Houston Museum of Fine Arts. The museum had required her father to hire an army of guards, one per every three paintings, to make sure the drunk people didn't touch the art.

She was a woman in love, and she had thought that was enough.

My talk about Jay had tired both of us out. I put Lucy down in her crib and stood watching her for a while. Then, when I'd had my fill of her face, and in it the shades of my best friend's face, I went out to the couch and closed my eyes to keep the tears shut in, and I stayed like that until I fell asleep, until I woke to hear Darrah and Daniel's car in the drive.

They opened the front door slowly, as if they were thieves, and they looked at me with questioning faces. Yes, I nodded, she's asleep. Daniel raised his arms in victory and then bent to kiss me on the cheek and to whisper, "God bless you." Darrah gave me a big hug, and we waved our silent good-byes and I tiptoed out of their house.

Remember the Alamo

One Sunday morning, sitting in the multidenominational campus church service, I felt a strong need to do some sort of penance for Alice Jamison's life. I hadn't been behind the wheel, drunk, of the car that ran her down, but I had been part of it. Jay and I were linked in this thing, in this drunken dance, and I couldn't undo it. Even if I never saw Jay again, I would still drag Alice Jamison's ruined life rattling behind me. My history would still include the night I spent with Heinz Fechtler, and the night I told Jay about it and he roared off on his deadly binge. My history would still include the many nights I had not said a word about Jay's drinking, the early phase of our marriage when he had been drunk but still paid attention to me so I hadn't cared as much. My life would still include the years when I thought I could fix Jay like I fixed my ballplayers, when I thought I could tutor him in sobriety as if it were a foreign language, when I didn't yet know it was up to him, and up to me, to be the best versions of our separate selves that we could be.

I signed up for Meals on Wheels, which I could do in the mornings while my athletes were in class. In the training session they told us to be observant of the clients' living spaces, to watch out, for example, for people with no air-conditioning who refused to open their windows for fear of burglars. We were to gently encourage these people to open their windows, even just a crack. We were to warn them, but not obnoxiously, about the many elderly Texans who died of heat exhaustion every year in their tightly sealed, unair-conditioned apartments.

I volunteered to do recording for the blind, where I read aloud textbooks on Texas history, our gory, bloody history. I read about the Alamo with its walls three feet thick, how it sheltered a hundred and eighty-nine Texans during Santa Ana's thirteen-day siege, how, by the end, every last Alamo defender was dead except for sixteen women and children. The textbook script didn't specify how many of the sixteen were women and how many were children. I don't know why it didn't tell, and for some reason I very much wanted to know. I wanted to know whether the other people in the Meals on Wheels meetings and the Recording for the Blind sound booths were survivors of some siege as well, if they were simply nice people or if they were, like me, stumbling through their good deeds with the desperate hope of scrubbing out a bad one. I wanted to know if they, like me, ever felt the urge to scream, "Come on already . . . *forget* the Alamo!"

I filled up every minute of my free time with volunteer work, and when I couldn't commit to any more scheduled work, I started dropping by the houses of my Meals on Wheels clients at odd times, to help them with their errands, to take the edge off their loneliness, and mine. I particularly liked the difficult clients, the demanding old ladies who made me feel I was earning my keep on this earth. That's why I went by to check on Mrs. Kelsey on the hottest day of September, in the midst of a record heat wave. She greeted me with "My, it's a warm one, isn't it? And you know why, young lady? It's the heat generated from all these air conditioners, that's what it is. If everyone would turn off their air-conditioning, the temperature would drop a good ten degrees, my hand to God. When I was a girl we didn't have this kind of heat. A good screen porch and an attic fan was all you needed back then."

I headed straight for the kitchen and moved aside the Verse-A-Day calendar to open the window above the sink. I didn't look to see what the verse of the day was, whether it was a nice one like "You will be like a well-watered garden, like a spring whose waters never fail," or one of those guilt-inducing ones about horsemen coming to get me, to drag me into a lake of fire.

"Mrs. Kelsey," I said, wrenching the window open, "you could have a heatstroke in here."

"Faith!" Mrs. Kelsey said, resting a light, dry hand on my arm to stop me, a hand with the force of a small moth. "Haven't you heard about the South Austin rapist? He attacks single women in ground-floor apartments who leave their windows open."

I looked at Mrs. Kelsey's face, trenched with wrinkles, at her hunched upper body that had swallowed her breasts, at her yellow-white helmet hair that the heat had melted to resemble a bathing cap more than a helmet. The old woman's eyes were bright with interest and fear. I couldn't stand to dim them by telling her she was in the wrong decade, that the South Austin rapist had long since been caught.

"That's right!" I said, taking her hand from the hot sill.

"I'd completely forgotten. Well, what are we going to do to get you out of this heat? Ice cream?"

"It's fine, Hope," Mrs. Kelsey said. She often confused my name, changing it to Hope or Charity. "It gets better after five o'clock. Now tell me how you are. How are those hired thugs who beat you all the time?"

"My football players? They're not real thugs," I said. "I just call them that, as a joke. They're just boys. Big boys, and they certainly don't beat me. Actually, my boss would strangle me if he heard me calling them hired thugs. We're supposed to call them 'student-athletes.'" In that sweltering apartment, I felt that my skin was melting off my bones. It was late afternoon. I needed to be in the study lounge by seven, when the athletes would be back from dinner. But I had time to take Mrs. Kelsey to get some ice cream. I had the idea that ice cream would fix everything.

"A good beating never hurt anyone," Mrs. Kelsey said, leaning against the kitchen counter. The counter was covered with used paper towels, spread out to dry so they could be put back to work. I thought I could see a cloud of humidity concentrated over the moist white squares. This and the talk of rape and beating seemed to raise the temperature in the room even higher, until I imagined I saw the English ivy in the wallpaper pattern wilting and drooping. I fought the urge to water it. I thought of how baseball *sounds* so much nicer than football, how football is full of sickening, crushing noises.

"Mrs. Kelsey," I said, "why don't I drive us down the street and we'll get some ice cream? Wouldn't you like to cool off for a few minutes?"

"You poor thing," Mrs. Kelsey said, looking me up and

down. "Of course the child wants some ice cream. Children love ice cream, don't they?"

"Yes, they do," I said. I loved it when Mrs. Kelsey called me "the child." I went over to her house time after time, pretending to care for her, asking after her health and feeding her awful food, all for the moments when she treated me like I was four years old.

I cupped her scrawny elbow in my palm and steered her through the hot tunnel of her apartment to find her purse and the clear plastic bonnet she wore over her hair rain or shine. My fingers were damp when I tried to get the slippery white plastic straps of the bonnet fastened under the old woman's chin without snagging that thin, loose skin, skin that seemed to have lost all structure. Although I was actually slim, I felt plump next to Mrs. Kelsey. I felt ripe, delicious. I schemed to turn the conversation again to a subject that would cause her to call me "the child." I missed my mother, but I wasn't ready to call her up and say, "Mother, I need you desperately." Instead I scattered my energy among strangers, or spent it writing lies to Tonía: "Everything here is fabulous! My husband just added a wing on to his dental clinic with a special waiting room full of toys for little girls like you. Are you taking good care of your teeth? As the sign in my husband's office says, 'You Don't Have to Floss All Your Teeth, Just the Ones You Want to Keep!'"

"My father didn't talk much, you know," Mrs. Kelsey said. "He let his belt do his talking for him."

"What kind of ice cream are you going to have today?" I said, steering her out the door and down the AstroTurfed front steps. Mrs. Kelsey's dress where I touched it at the elbow was damp with sweat. I knew she was having one of her bad days. I knew the ice cream place would be a trial, the choice of flavors a confusion to this elderly woman who'd grown up in a small Texas town where the only ice cream available was what people made themselves.

I almost hoped for a bad day. I almost hoped Mrs. Kelsey would spill her vanilla ice cream all over my T-shirt, that she'd urinate on the floor of the ice cream parlor and I would have to scrub it up in front of the disgusted teenage staff and the fleeing customers. I almost hoped the South Austin rapist would burst out of jail and find his way through Mrs. Kelsey's windows, that I'd rescue her at great personal cost. Then I'd go back to the dorms, saturated with heat and sorrow. But I would have stored up some good deeds, a shield of good deeds against the past, against the ever-present image of Alice Jamison that not even the hottest Texas afternoon could melt away.

Preventive Medicine

Sometimes, late at night in my dorm room, it struck me that Jay and I were living in spaces of roughly the same size, that we both slept on single beds, that we both used furniture that was bolted to the floor. Then I'd get up and wander around the halls, checking on my football players, lecturing any available linebackers about how even though they were rewarded for violence on the field, they weren't going to be rewarded for it anywhere else. This was preventive medicine, my attempt to avoid wrecked hotel rooms, barroom brawls, domestic violence and assault charges.

"Yeah, yeah," they'd say. "Okay, Miss Evers, we get it." These were boys who routinely yelled, "Blood makes the grass grow; kill, kill, kill!" I felt justified in repeating myself as much as possible.

In between pep talks, I'd go down to the poolroom and play a video game or two, letting myself get annihilated over and over. Some nights I'd talk someone into going for a run with me, sometimes Cam McClure but more often Hub Owen. Hub was a wide receiver, accustomed to bursts of speed, quick accelerations, but not long distances. We slumped on the steps of the dorm one night after running seven or eight miles, Hub saying, "Miss Evers, you kicked my ass, man."

"I wouldn't kick your ass in a sprint, honey."

"Yeah, maybe not," he said, cheering up. He squeezed half the water from his orange plastic bottle over his head. "Hey, Miss Evers," he said.

"What's that, Hub?"

"This is kinda embarrassing, you know, but . . ."

"What is it, babe?"

"Would you help me, you know, make up a dance?"

"What do you mean?" I said. I looked at his military-short hair, the ends damp and sharp in the moonlight. I imagined scrubbing something with it.

"You know, for when I catch touchdowns. I want something to be my, you know . . ."

"Your signature?"

"Yeah, that's it."

"Okay, well, do you want it to be a dance you do with another player or by yourself?"

"By myself, I guess, 'cause, you know, I don't really want to ask anyone else, you know. But it's gotta be good, Miss Evers, or, you know, the black guys'll give me shit."

"Honey, Eddie and Drew don't have the market cornered on coolness. There's still room for you, all right? They're gonna wish they had moves like you, darlin'."

I jumped down off the steps and started wiggling my legs and hips as if I were being electrocuted by the ghost of Elvis Presley. I jumped up in the air and pretended to catch a pass, my technique for which had Hub leaning over on one elbow, helpless with laughter, then I came up with a move that was part disco, part Elvis.

"Well?" I said.

When Hub was able to talk he said, "I don't know, Miss Evers. Maybe something a little more, you know . . ."

"Subtle?"

"Yeah, that's it. Subtle."

"Well, I'm not a stage show, sweetie. You get down here and help me."

We worked on it for a while, even surviving the moment when Cam McClure leaned out his window and yelled, "What're y'all doin' down there?" and Hub dove under an Indian hawthorn bush.

"We're stretching!" I yelled up at Cam. "Did you finish that chapter?"

That got rid of him.

Hub crawled out from under the bush and I said, "Honey, remember that you're going to be doing this in front of fifty thousand people, and that's not even counting the TV audience."

"I can do it, Miss Evers," he said, and I said, "That's the spirit," and we finally came up with something not at all reminiscent of disco but a little Elvis, a hint of Fred Astaire, and a touch of yoga. Hub went upstairs to get a football and I tossed it to him a few times so he could practice with the ball in his hands. It was two in the morning, long past lights-out, but I was so happy to be distracted from my troubles that I kept on throwing, kept on cheering Hub's dance.

"Thanks, Miss Evers," Hub said when he finally had it down, when I'd thrown him pass after pass without him once saying I threw like a girl, and I was sorry it was over.

Back in my room, I knew I wouldn't be able to sleep and I thought about going for another run, then thought how crazy that was. I ended up taking Jay's letters and cutting the good parts out of them, the parts that could have been written from a husband on a very long business trip, and I taped them to the inside of the fake wood door of my closet.

"Buddy," read one of the closet sections, "with you as my magnetic *N*, Buddy, I keep moving toward the possibility of redemption and happiness, toward the day when I can start my education again, a long course of studying and savoring your body, your being. I want to walk with you. I want to eat with you. I want to take you home and lay you down and tell you how much I love you. I want to take responsibility for the shitty things I've done and make sure you know I will never do them again."

I filled in the gaps with bits of Tonía's letters: "Dear Faith, I wish I could come to your house and jump on your trampoline. I can do a back flip. My friend Angie can do a back one and a front one. We do them at the pool. My mom takes us there on Wednesdays. I wish today was Wednesday."

The parts of Jay's letters that didn't make it to the closet said things like this: "One of my cellmates, a kid named Michael, lived in Austin for a while. Went to UT until he got strung out on boy (heroin). The slang for coke is girl and when people do a speedball they say they did a boy and a girl. Just a little drug lingo for your edification, Buddy." Or this: "It seems like I've been waiting forever to get into the work program, but first TDC has to verify that I have indeed graduated from high school. Otherwise, I'd have to work on my GED instead of going into town and picking up trash for four hours a day. I can't wait to go into town and pick up trash, Buddy, and I mean that. I can't wait to smell the outdoors, to see normal people walking around doing normal things, to have a job and to do it. Although when I think about my high school being contacted by the TDC, sometimes I think I'd rather just pretend I'm a dropout and work on my stupid GED." Or this: "I am so fucking bored and the book cart doesn't come again until Tuesday. I don't know if it's someone's idea of a sick joke, but most of their titles have something to do with jail. Last week I got Vonnegut's *Jailbird* and Sartre's *No Exit*. By the way, I'm almost out of envelopes and I won't get to 'make store,' as they say in here, until Saturday, so there might be a lull in these fascinating letters of mine."

When I had finished butchering Jay's letters, I went down to the janitor's closet for a broom and a mop and I swept my floor and mopped myself out into the hallway; then I sat there on the floor, wishing one of my athletes would be jolted awake with a sudden desire to cram some information into his thick head, with a burning need to crank out a draft of a paper. Anything to keep open the door to my room, to remind myself of the fundamental difference between our two prisons: I could walk away from mine. Finally I walked back into my very clean room and did Hub's dance a couple of times in front of the mirror. I did it until I recaptured a hint of the fun we'd had making it up, then I dove under the covers and willed myself into sleep, gripping that shred of happiness like you'd grip the string of a kite let loose in a great, roaring wind.

You Could End Up Living in a Trailer

On the Saturdays when the Longhorns had away games, I drove to Dayton to see my husband live and in person. I wasn't obligated to go to the home games, but I felt it helped my rapport with the hired thugs, and it was easier for me to keep a grip on their attitudes toward their schoolwork when I could observe their attitudes on the football field. And sometimes I welcomed the chance to scream my heart out.

On the weekends when I drove to Dayton, I sped right past the exit to my parents' house. I had spoken with Daddy once since Jay's arrest, long enough for him to tell me that Jay's earning power would be greatly reduced post-prison, that there would be a hideous blank spot of at least two and a half years, perhaps more, on his résumé and was I considering a divorce. Mother picked up the other phone and said, "Honey, how are you? Do you need anything?"

Well, yes, I could have said. *I need to invent a new version of myself to go with my newly sober husband. We need to invent a new version of our marriage. I need to think up some things to say to Jay besides, "Honey, please don't. Jay, haven't you had enough? I wish you wouldn't, sweetheart."*

"No," I said, joyfully. "I'm fine." I was so happy she had asked that I hardly heard what she said next.

"Well, grand. Now, Faith, I know you don't want to hear it from me, but Sugar, if you stay married to Jay, you could end up living in a *trailer*. People who've been in prison live in trailers, you know, and there's no place to have a garden and you'll probably get blown away by a tornado."

"Claire, get off the phone," Daddy said.

"This isn't what we raised her for, Henry. This isn't what we sent her to private school all her life for."

"No one's invited me to live in a trailer, Mother."

"Well, good-bye then."

I didn't tell her I'd live in the most disgusting trailer in the world with Jay if he could stay sober.

When I visited Jay I was always surprised at how pale he was. I don't know why I chose something like that to be surprised about. I probably should have been more surprised by the fact that I was married to a convicted felon, to a man who slept on a plastic mattress and bought his toothpaste at a commissary, but I chose instead to be surprised by the paleness of Jay's skin, by its contrast to my own.

Our visits happened in a large concrete room with stainless steel picnic tables bolted to the floor. I thought the picnic tables were particularly cruel, with their images of parks, barbeques, happier times. We sat at the end of one, our thighs nearly touching but not quite; Jay, as a model prisoner, was allowed "contact visits," which meant we could hug and exchange a kiss at the beginning and end of each visit, but we weren't supposed to touch beyond that. Depending on which guard was assigned to supervise our group of tables, we sometimes slipped in an extra touch, a brush of our arms against each other, brief and furtive and nearly exotic. But most of the time we sat without touching and tried to tune out the racket of the other fifty couples in the room, everyone trying to put their four-hour visit to good use, to wreak as much love from it as they possibly could. We tried to ignore the ghost of Alice Jamison, although her name was written plainly on our faces, in the new wrinkle in Jay's forehead, in the lines at the corners of my eyes. When Jay asked me what I'd been doing, I explicitly did not tell him about my friendship with Richard Jamison. I left out the phone conversations, the gallons and gallons of salsa, the times we walked around Town Lake and went from talking about how much we missed our spouses to comparing notes on the things about them that had driven us crazy. I left out the times I talked about Jay as if he were dead.

"How're the hired thugs?" Jay asked me one fall Saturday. I told him about my football players, about their humiliating loss to UCLA, about how Gary Ecco, the quarterback, had confided in me that this loss was the worst thing that had happened to him in his whole entire life.

"Must be nice," Jay said.

"Yeah," I said. I think we both would have given anything to be able to say that the worst thing that had ever happened to us was losing a football game.

"How're D and D?" Jay said. "Or I guess I should say D, D, and L?"

"They're okay," I said, thinking of the lunch I'd had with Darrah earlier in the week, when she'd told me no one would blame me for divorcing Jay. *I've put up with Jay's drinking all this time,* I told her. *I'm not giving up my chance to have him sober.* We'd spent the rest of the lunch talking baby talk to Lucy, unable to think of anything to say to each other.

"My friend C.P.," Jay said abruptly, "and I use the word 'friend' loosely, he's been in here two years and he's never had a visitor. He's got family, but he can't deal with going through the strip search. Told his people to stay away."

"Do you want me to stay away?"

"Of course not, Buddy. I don't know why I told you that. Just making conversation. I'd go through a hundred searches to see you for thirty seconds. I mean it. So, tell me what you've been reading. What kind of music you've been listening to."

"I bought the new Antonio Hart," I managed to say. Then I put my head down on the picnic table and Jay lifted a hand to touch my shoulder and then thought better of it. I didn't want to cry. In general, I tried to be cheerful during our visits, to save my crying for the long drive home. But sometimes I couldn't hold on that long, and this was one of those times. I cried all over the bolted-down picnic table and its shiny, dented surface.

"Buddy," Jay whispered. "Oh, Buddy, I'm so sorry. I'm so sorry it's come to this." He said those things over and over, whispering them deep into my ear without letting his mouth actually touch my skin, and then, "Buddy, is it too much for you? Do you want out?"

Then I cried more as the answer to his question surfaced in my heart, as I knew that what I wanted was not to get away from Jay and his problems but to sleep in his arms every single night, to wake up with him every morning, and to go through my day knowing he'd be at the end of it. It took me a while to stop crying, to gather my voice into one coherent thing.

"No," I said, willing it to be true. "I want in."

This Academic Bullshit

UT was supposed to have a good football team that fall. A number of sportswriters had picked us to win the Big 12 Championship. The Associated Press preseason poll ranked us at number 8. Gordon Riley, our star running back, had agreed to give us one more year before turning pro. Gary Ecco, the starting quarterback, was a senior and aching for a championship. And we were the only school to rank in the top twenty-five in all four major offensive categories: rushing, passing, scoring, and total offense.

Three weeks into the season, the best thing about the team was that nobody was failing any classes yet. Three humiliating losses, two of them exciting the other team's fans to tear down the goalposts, and we dropped out of the AP poll altogether. The media called daily for Coach Walston's resignation. His wife, a tiny gold longhorn skull strung around her neck, screamed her lungs out in the coaches' wives' section the day we were slowly crushed by Oklahoma State.

The good news was that none of it was my fault. I cheered, nagged, lectured, and sympathized. I wore my horrible burnt orange clothing stamped with white longhorn skulls and marched out to pep rallies. I sang "The Eyes of

Texas" at top volume whenever necessary. I let a sobbing Gary Ecco rest his big, heavy, neckless head on my shoulder until the blood flow to my arm stopped entirely. I longed for the relative peace of baseball season. I wrote Tonía extravagant lies about how well my team was doing, as if she couldn't hear on television how awful they were, as if it wasn't common knowledge that my boys were failing miserably. I told my hired thugs they were still kicking ass in the Game of Life.

Two days after my boys blew an early lead to Missouri, the defensive coordinator called me into his office. The walls were covered in chalkboards that in turn were marked with frenzied little circles and arrows. Harry sat at his desk, behind a rough landscape of playbooks, scouting reports, and newspapers mourning our slump.

"What can I do for you, Harry?" I said. I entertained myself by staring at the bald spot the size of a silver dollar on the peak of his head. Usually Harry avoided me, because I had repeatedly begged him to stop calling his players "a fuckin' *woman*" and "you *goddamn lady*" when they missed a tackle or played as if they were not quite as full of testosterone as Harry thought they ought to be.

"Faith," he said. "Things are falling apart here. And I get the feeling — now, correct me if I'm wrong — that our student-athletes are just, well, *distracted* by all these tests and papers and, you know, all this academic bullshit."

"That's the 'student' part of 'student-athlete,' Harry."

"Yeah, yeah, I know. Hey, I've got a degree myself."

"Good for you."

"But what I'm saying is, and Coach Walston and the other assistants and I have all agreed on this, and they asked me to talk to you about it, is that we think you're doing your job a little too well. Now, I know you're proud of the jump in the student-athletes' GPAs during your time here, and we're proud of it, too, but we were just thinking that if you backed off some, I mean, keep them eligible, for Chrissakes, but free them up some so they can concentrate more on their game."

"Harry, how many boys in this program do you expect to make it to the NFL?"

"Now, I know what you're getting at, Faith. I know everyone's not a Riley or an Ecco, but what I'm saying is —"

"Harry, I want these boys to have something to fall back on when they realize they're not all going to be doing Nike commercials, or when they get injured, or when they're thirty and their bodies are so battered they have to retire. I think we need to shoot for more than just having them graduate. I want them to graduate with honors. I want their GPAs to be up there. Look at Lewis Jones, for example. Sports management major, but he's smart enough to do better. He's a decent lineman but he'll never make it in the pros, am I right?" Harry nodded. "What if he matures some and decides to live up to his potential, decides he wants to go on to grad school or law school? And what if he's hampered in that effort because we decided it was enough just to keep him eligible, just to get him through his seasons and if we're lucky on to graduation?"

Harry gripped his forehead with the index finger and thumb of one hand in a you're-giving-me-a-headache gesture. His bald spot seemed to contract slightly. "You're saying he could sue."

"No! I'm not saying he could sue! All anyone thinks about

around here is what kind of lawsuits they might get nailed with. I'm saying it's wrong. It's just plain wrong."

"Look, Faith, I know you're good at what you do. Bob Talwen raved about your work during baseball season. But baseball . . . it's just not as big a deal and you know it. We've got the whole state breathing down our necks, Faith; the goddamn governor wants to know what the hell's going on over here! Look, the bottom line is Walston wants the study area closed down at ten thirty instead of eleven thirty, give the boys an extra hour of sleep and see if it helps over the next couple of weeks. Can you live with that?"

"He's the boss," I said.

"I know you don't like it, but that's the way it is."

"Hook 'em, Horns," I said.

Chocolate

While my football players stumbled through loss after loss, the usually awful Chicago Cubs squeaked into a one-game playoff with the San Francisco Giants that fall, and Richard Jamison invited me over to watch it. I've had a standing hatred for the Giants ever since they crushed my Cubs in the 1989 NLCS, but my hatred had softened slightly because Micah was pitching for them. All my athletes were excited about it; even Coach Talwen, as angry as he'd been, admitted that he was "interested," although he did want to know how a native Texan like myself ended up a Cubs fan.

"My mother loves the ivy at Wrigley," I told him. "She brainwashed me from birth."

"I hear you," Coach said.

I was terrified of going to Richard's house, the house where he'd lived with Alice.

"I don't know," I told him on the phone. We'd always met at restaurants, outside movie theaters, in bright, public places.

"Come on," Richard said. "You know what it's like to be a baseball fan marooned in Texas. Every time I turn on the TV there's a broadcast of a high school football game. High school! Come over and sympathize with me. Plus, the Cubs'll probably get killed and then I'll really need sympathy."

"Spoken like a true Cubs fan," I said. Richard had grown up in Chicago. "What should I bring?"

"Everything," he said. "Anything. My fridge hasn't seen food in months. I might as well unplug it."

"I'll see what I can do," I said.

Sometimes Maya, the head cook, would let me come over to the cafeteria and bake cookies or a loaf of bread, when I was feeling extra homesick for a real kitchen. It was awkward to measure out a cup or two of flour into the huge mixer meant for pounds of flour, not cups, to bake my few little cookies on the giant trays in the industrial-size oven. Maya would sit on her stool and laugh at me; she'd tell me I could come over and help her cook two hundred pounds of barbeque for dinner that night, if I wasn't rid of my cooking urge yet. One day I baked a batch of peanut butter chocolate chip cookies and express-mailed them to Tonía in Oklahoma. I hoped her parents wouldn't think I was some kind of maniac, the sort of person who would stick razor blades in Halloween apples. Another day, near the end of baseball season, I baked three trays of fudge for my ballplayers, hoping to take the edge off an embarrassing series sweep at the hands of the hated Sooners, which had followed on the heels of a series sweep by Baylor, both Big 12 teams my darlings had once dominated.

The day I walked over to bake a tray of brownies to take to Richard's, we couldn't even find a baking pan small enough to accommodate my recipe. Finally I decided to quadruple the recipe and to leave the extras in the study lounge for the hired thugs.

"You got a date?" Maya said. "A *novio?*" Maya wore long cornrows into which she'd woven various things: a pair of dice, a small plastic bluebird, a rhinestone ring, a tiny cowbell. Her hair clanked and jangled as she talked.

"No tengo novio," I told her. *"Tengo esposo."* I don't have a boyfriend. I have a husband.

"Ay," Maya said, and I could see her wondering why I lived in the dorm by myself, why I ate most of my meals in the cafeteria with boys whose body weight was nearly three times my own.

"My husband's in prison," I said. Sometimes I made myself tell people, made myself say it aloud even in the privacy of my room, just to hear the truth of it.

Maya nodded, her face sinking from a smile into hard, settled lines.

I told her about the accident, about Jay's drinking. I cracked eggs into my dark brownie batter and watched them disappear.

"I will pray for him," she said, crossing herself. "And for you."

"Thank you, Maya," I said, and I felt intensely grateful. I felt I could use as many prayers as she was willing to pray.

Later, when Richard opened his front door and I offered him my tray of homemade brownies, he immediately stuffed one in his mouth and started making noises of appreciation. When he could talk again, he said, "God, where would we be without chocolate? It's the best. These brownies are the best. Do you think you could possibly cram a little more chocolate in these things? Can I have them all?"

I felt so happy that he liked chocolate. Jay would tolerate it, and he was happy to provide me with as much of it as I wanted, but he didn't crave it the way I did. He didn't really *get* it. If he had his way, he'd rather have an apple pie or a peach cobbler, or maybe a cheesecake, whereas I'd never waste my time on a nonchocolate dessert.

That was the first time I had that sort of thought, a thought in which I compared Richard to Jay and Richard came out more favorably. I didn't even realize it at the time. I just walked right into Richard's house and shoved aside the computer magazines on his coffee table to make room for the tray of brownies. We talked and ate and watched baseball and turned our caps sideways on our heads when the Cubs were in danger and crossed our fingers and toes when they had a chance to do something wonderful. During the commercials he showed me some pictures of Alice, taken on a weekend in Corpus Christi. When I started to cry a little about how my husband had killed this adorable girl in the red-and-white-striped bikini, Richard said, "Hey, Faith, maybe you could take a look at our garden sometime. It was pretty much Alice's deal and now I don't really know what to do with it." I told him I'd help him get it going again, that it would be better before he knew it. I think we were both incredibly attracted to anything we could make better; we were both ready to roll up our sleeves and go to work. We talked and watched and I said to the television several times, "Oh, Micah, I hate to root against you but you're a damn Giant, honey!" We sneered at the commercials and yelled encouragement to the Cubs until they finally, miraculously, won. We ate brownies until we were delirious, and I drove back to the dorms without marking that thought about the chocolate for what it was, without knowing what it meant.

She Wants Us to Think

Occasionally I still listened to the Mistress. I listened just enough to hear that she was still on the same track, that *bum* was still her favorite word, that she had a seizure when a caller mentioned his or her feelings: "We *must* stop worshiping the god of *feelings*," she ranted in her preacher's voice. "We don't make decisions based on *feelings*. We make our decisions based on a code of behavior. Ditch the feelings, all right?"

Sometimes I'd try to think up an answer to the question she had asked me, about why I would be attracted to such a person as Jay, but I fished for reasons as if I needed to fill in the blanks on a test; none of it came from my heart. Choose one and only one of the following options: Faith is attracted to Jay because (a) her father is an alcoholic, (b) she's a teacher and therefore sees room for improvement in everyone, (c) her childhood dog was named Jayboy, (d) all of the above, (e) none of the above.

When the Mistress wasn't on I kept my radio tuned to KGSR, the station my hired thugs liked to listen to when they crowded into my room late at night, after the maintenance man had, on Coach's orders, locked up the study lounge. They squeezed their huge bodies onto my furniture, kicked off their massive tennis shoes, and stretched out on my floor. They tried to talk under the sound of the radio in case Coach sent an assistant to do a lights-out check. *Miss Evers, Miss Evers, Miss Evers,* they whispered.

One night Gary slumped on the floor with a laptop balanced on his thighs, trying to write an outline for a paper on *Macbeth.* Jimmy Brosnan, our kicker, sat on my bed with his right foot as always sheathed in three layers of socks, so many socks that his right foot took one shoe size larger than his left. Hub Owen, who had not yet had a chance to show the world his dance because Gary had thrown far more interceptions than touchdowns, sat at the other end of my bed with a horticulture textbook open on his lap. Hub had confided in me before the semester started that he would easily kick ass in horticulture because he'd grown marijuana with his brothers during high school. I wouldn't believe, he told me, the *quality,* you know, of the *shit* they grew. This horticulture class was supposed to be Hub's ticket to fulfilling those elusive science requirements. Now he quivered on my bed, whispering, "Miss Evers, this fuckin' class, man. You gotta help me. You just gotta."

"What are you working on, Hub?"

"This take-home exam. The answers aren't in the book, Miss Evers. We're supposed to, you know, think them up."

"Radical, isn't it?"

"Come on, Miss Evers." Hub had, for the previous week's pep rally, painted his face orange and white, and the orange had not completely come out of his skin, in spite of the fact that his girlfriend had scrubbed it with a variety of reportedly *stinky* facial products. I tried not to laugh as I looked at his puzzled, strangely shadowed face.

"What's the first question, babe?" I said.

" 'Most gardeners treat trees as individuals, unaware that the roots of many trees cross each other's paths beneath the earth, some even growing together to form natural graft unions. What possible advantages might result from a tree joining its roots to those of another tree?' "

"And there's nothing about that in your book?"

"Nah, Miss Evers. She fuckin' told us the answers aren't in the book. She said she wants us to think."

"Well, I know it's torturous, but that's what you'll have to do."

"Isn't there some other way?"

"No, baby. Now listen. Did you ever play red rover when you were a kid?"

"Yeah, sometimes."

"Describe the game to me as if I come from a country where no one's ever heard of it."

"Miss Evers . . ."

"Come on, now. Just humor your poor old tutor."

"Okay, well, it's this game where a bunch of kids stand in a line and hold hands, or really you're not holding hands but you sorta hold each other's forearms, you know, you get a chain of kids all joined together at the arms. Then there's a line of kids across from you, maybe twenty yards away or something, and someone on one side yells, 'Red rover, red rover, let John,' or whoever the fuck, 'come over.' You pick a kid from the other side and call out his name. Then that kid comes hauling ass over, and you try to hold your line firm, and he tries to break through it, you know."

"Okay, so imagine that the line of kids is a line of trees. What sort of thing might be a threat to trees as far as breaking them, knocking them over?"

"I don't know. Wind, I guess. Tornado. This your daughter?" he said, picking up a photo of Tonía I kept on the windowsill, her school photo with a marbled blue background and her mouth crammed with braces.

"I don't have a daughter. I'm too busy with you guys. Now, pay attention, Hub. Do you think a line of trees with their roots grafted together would have a better chance of withstanding wind than a bunch of trees with individual roots?"

"You think?"

"I'm asking you, Hub."

He thought about it while Gary whispered, "Miss Evers! Could you look at my outline in a sec?"

"Okay," Hub said. "I guess they would have a better chance, you know, cause they'd have like this network of roots that would be stronger and bigger than the individual tree's roots."

"So there you go. That's one advantage to trees grafting their roots to each other. Think you can translate that into written English?"

"Hopefully," Hub said, smiling.

"What did you say, young man?" I said, grabbing his arm and twisting it behind his back.

"Ow! I'm just kidding, Miss Evers. Hey! I need that arm for catching, you know?"

I let him go and walked over and sat next to Gary and

looked at what he'd written on the laptop screen. Then I tried to think up a nice way to tell him he needed to do better.

"Okay," I said. "You know how sometimes in football you run a play that's actually very simple but you do something to try to make the other team think it's more complicated?"

"I'm with you."

"Well, you've got the right idea here with your thesis sentence, 'Macbeth was pussy-whipped by his wife,' but we need to make it sound a little more complex than that. And we need to dump the p-word, definitely, unless you want me to slap you silly. Try to think about Macbeth's character in terms of things that were already within him that made it easy for his wife to convince him to do whatever she wanted. You know what I mean? Did she take a very strong man and tear him down or did she take a man with weak spots and exploit those?"

"So my prof is the other team."

"Miss Evers" came a whisper from across the room.

"Hold on, Jones," I said. "You want to think about it for a minute and I'll be right back?" I asked Gary.

"Yeah, okay."

The phone rang and I answered it without any hope that it might be the person I most wanted to talk to; the Texas prison system was one of the few that didn't allow outgoing phone calls, although the phone company was always lobbying for a change in rules because they wanted all those potential collect call revenues. It was Richard, saying, "Hey, I know it's late, but I just, I don't know."

"It's not too late," I said. "I'm still working, actually, and then I was thinking of going for a run."

"Don't run, Faith. Running bounces your internal organs around; it's a well-known medical fact. Come out and have some caffeine and smoke some cigarettes with me. I can't sleep. I'm going kind of stir-crazy over here. I've even resorted to lifting weights."

"See, you're not as unhealthy as you pretend to be."

"It's strictly sanity maintenance. So . . ."

"I'm not going to be free for a while, but if you want to wait . . ."

"Do you want to just call me when you're done?"

"Sure, I'll do that."

When I hung up the phone, all my thugs were staring at me.

"What?" I said.

"Who was that?" Hub said. "A guy?"

"None of your business," I said. "Get back to your horticulture before I kick your butt out of here." To avoid their eyes, I walked over to my window and opened it, then stood there and let the warm fall breeze cover my arms and face. The air was so warm I could have pretended, if I wished, that we hadn't yet had a change of season since Jay left. But I was beginning to court the passage of time, the possibility of violent change, the idea that life would never again be as I had known it. Lucy would never again be the age she was when I knew her best: three months old and fascinated with her hands, holding her little hands in front of her face and gazing at them as if she didn't realize they were attached to her body, as if they were clouds, or UFOs. I would never again try to pretend Jay wasn't drunk, make excuses to myself for the fact that he was drunk, or offer to mix him a drink with the idea that I wouldn't make it nearly as strong as he would. My life was going to be different, and every breath of October air told me so.

My boys slowly turned back to their work, but I was left with a residue of guilt about Richard. By the time Gary had expanded his vision of Macbeth, Hub had finished his take-home exam, and Jones had written an essay in Spanish about the athletic spirit on and off the field, by the time I was sitting across from Richard on the porch of the all-night coffee shop, I felt I was sneaking around on Jay somehow. I hadn't told him about Richard, because I just didn't quite know how to say, "I'm friends with the husband of the woman you killed." I had told Tonía, my pen pal. I had written to her: "I have a nice friend named Richard who works with computers. He likes to eat Mexican food, although sometimes his eyes water when the food is too spicy. Does that ever happen to you?"

"Thanks for coming out," Richard said. "All my other friends have kids and I can't even call them after like nine o'clock."

"I know what you mean," I said, thinking of Darrah. "So, you're having a hard night."

"Yeah," he said. He stabbed out one cigarette and lit another. "Cancer stick?"

"No, thanks."

"You know, sometimes I go along for two or three days and I'm okay, but then other days it's like every minute is a day and every thought that goes through my head is water torture."

"I know," I said. "Sometimes I stay awake all night hoping one of my athletes will knock on my door and need help with a paper or something. I mean, sometimes they do and then I just turn off my heart and go into my teacher mode and it's such a relief. I can see why people become workaholics. I'd bet you anything that inside every workaholic there's a broken heart."

"I believe it," Richard said. His glasses were smudged. I reached across the table, pulled them off his face, cleaned them with the end of my shirt, and set them back on his ears. "Thank you," he said.

It felt strange to be out late at night with a man who wasn't Jay. I didn't know the layers and layers of this man. I didn't know exactly how many home runs Richard had hit in Little League and which members of his family had been present for each. I didn't know about his elementary school triumphs and griefs, about the time he was nine and found his older brother's bong hidden under the steps in the basement, how he ran to his brother and said, "I know what that is! That's a *bog!*" and his brother fell over laughing. I didn't know if Richard's father was, like Jay's, certain to say after a long filibuster of advice-giving, "Now, don't mind me, I'm just being an old Polonius." I had no idea what sort of advice Richard's father gave, or whether his mother, like Jay's mother, responded to our thank-yous for Christmas money always with the same comment: "Well, I *thought* green was your color!" I didn't know whether he had been comforted by a Snoopy, a baba, a bankie, or a Pooh. I wasn't aware of this man's early loves, of the books that first made him want to read more books, of the records that caused him to hold an imaginary mike to his lips and pretend to be a disc jockey, of the first time he listened to a Jimi Hendrix album stoned and heard something completely different from what he had heard before. I didn't know exactly what Richard had been doing during certain Important Baseball Moments: Had he stood on his couch and yelled in happiness and thrown beer at the ceiling on purpose when Kirk Gibson hit his home run in 1988? Had he died a thousand deaths the day the ball rolled through Buckner's legs? I didn't know which Wallace Stevens poem was Richard's favorite, which P. G. Wodehouse books made him laugh the hardest, what his voice sounded like saying over and over for our amusement, "Mrs. Ulgine Barrows. That's *Ulgine*, Buddy. You're gorgeous and I'm ulgine. He has the dreaded cancer of the ulgine. Waiter, there's an ulgine in my soup!"

"You know," Richard said. "I stay up all night remembering Alice but I'm already starting to forget parts of her."

"I feel the same way about . . . I feel the same way," I said, as our conversation bumped up against a familiar obstacle, the big brick wall garishly graffitied with the words "Your Spouse Is Dead and Mine Isn't!"

"Tell me what you're forgetting," I said.

Richard brushed his hair back from his face. "I don't know," he said. "Things she told me that I wasn't paying much attention to because I figured I'd hear them again. Stories about her childhood, dreams she'd had. When I first started spending a lot of time on the computer she'd talk my ears off while I was trying to figure something out — I think back then she just saw it as another version of TV watching or something — and I'd just completely tune her out and focus in on the thing I was trying to do. I used to be so relieved when she'd go to sleep. It was like, *ahhh*, a couple of hours alone on the computer. And now," he said, "I have the rest of my life to be alone with my computers and I want to smash every last one of them."

"I know," I said, mournfully thinking of the time, before any of it had become a problem, when I'd playfully attached a note to Jay's little bong that read, "Jason, we know all about this bog. Love, the DEA."

I didn't have any old jokes with Richard, nothing that resonated, no catchwords or signals that spoke to him parts of our history. I couldn't say to him in my smallest voice, "Coe," and have him know that meant I was cold and needed him to wrap me in his arms and hold me until his body heat warmed me, until I was reminded of all the times he'd taken care of me that way, until I remembered that those times were part of what kept the undertow of his drunkenness from pulling me down. I looked at Richard and thought he was a good person, a smart and wonderful man whom I might have loved if we'd met ten years earlier, but now I didn't have time. I didn't have time to invent a new language with him, and to learn how to speak it.

"What are you thinking about?" Richard said.

"Nothing," I said.

Limes

My father had a heart attack the week after the Longhorns lost in a blowout to Texas Tech. He had just come home from the hospital and was mixing himself a highball in the form of a vodka and tonic and had started telling Mother how he'd reattached the arm of a man who had severed it in a tree-trimming accident. It was unusual for Daddy to tell Mother about his surgeries; he'd never quite forgiven her for the time she'd watched him perform an emergency appendectomy and exclaimed, "Well, Henry, I think *I* could do that! It's all just cutting and tying knots and stitching! It's really just sewing!"

But perhaps the tree-trimming aspect of it had drawn him past his grudge and toward my mother; surely he'd known she'd have an opinion as to whether it was the right time of year for trimming trees in the first place, at what angle the cuts should be made and what should be used to seal up the wounds. *Those wounds need to be sealed up right away,* I can just hear her saying.

He had turned to my mother and said, "Do we have any —" and then had collapsed. Mother attacked him with

CPR, learned years ago when I was small, until the ambulance came shrieking up to the house.

Do we have any limes? is what Mother thought he was probably trying to ask. "I think he'll be all right, Faith, but why don't you come just in case," she said. "If you think you can stand me, that is."

During the half hour it took me to pack for Houston, I must have picked up the phone four or five times to call Jay. I wasn't yet ready to write it down, to write, "Dear Jay, my father had a heart attack late last night and I'm going to Houston in a couple of hours. Wish you were here." I wanted to blurt it out on the telephone, to cry and sob and whine into the receiver and then to quiet down to hear him say, "Oh, Buddy, I'm so sorry." I dialed Richard's number but hung up before it started ringing. I felt if I talked to him, if he ended up being the one who listened to me cry, who said something comforting, it would draw me over a line I didn't want to cross. I also had a strong desire to bake an apple pie. I thought if I showed up at Mother's with a beautiful apple pie, that would somehow help us like each other again.

"Apples?" Maya said when I went down to the kitchen and managed to put the words together. "Sure we got apples. For a pie you need Granny Smith. I made a pie with Delicious one time, it was terrible. But I got my crew coming in fifteen minutes to start on dinner. Tonight, maybe?"

"Yeah, maybe," I said, knowing I'd be in Houston by then. "Thanks, Maya."

On my way back to the dorms I ran into Cory Bell, who said, "Miss Evers! Do you think you could . . . ?"

"I can't, honey, and you know it. I have to focus on the

football players." It was always difficult to wean my athletes off of me and into the "off-season" tutoring program. They whimpered at me like puppies, and I felt a mother's pull toward them. "You could do something for me, though," I said, thinking of something that might make him happy.

"What's that, Miss Evers?"

"You could say a prayer for my dad. He's in the hospital."

"Really, Miss Evers? You really want me to pray for him?"

"Couldn't hurt, could it?"

Cory dropped to his knees, right there in the grass, never mind all the students walking by with their see-through bookbags and their soy-milk lattes and their tiny headphones jammed deep into their severely pierced ears, never mind the ones who snickered at the message on Cory's T-shirt: "Make Your Eternal Reservations Now — In the Non-Smoking Section."

He folded his big hands and said, "Lord, our tutor, Miss Evers, she's just such a great example of how You work in mysterious ways, Lord. She's always sayin' this stuff about You, like how she's not about to believe in a God that has a penis and stuff like that, but here she's asked me to pray for her dad. I ask that You be with him in his time of trouble, Lord, that You just help him through this sickness, if that's Your will, Lord, and that these problems will draw Miss Evers's family closer together and closer to You, Lord. Amen."

I gave him a hand up. "How was that?" he said.

"You're the best, Cory," I said. "Thanks."

When I went back upstairs and called Richard and told him about my dad he said, "I'm coming over."

"Don't," I said. "I'm just packing and then I'm out of here."

"I'm coming over," he said again, and this time I didn't say no.

I sat on the edge of my bed and looked at my little suit-case, part of a set Jay's aunt Nikki had given us when we married.

I flipped open Jay's black spiral notebook and read Hang-over Cure #112, called in by a listener from Wimberly: "Okay, what you do is just go with it. I like to get up and do some aerobics or maybe run a couple of miles, then come back and spend some time talking to God on his white porce-lain telephone. It's really the only way."

I tried to imagine the day as it would have been if Jay had been part of it: I would have been home, in our house, when Mother called to tell me the news. Grace would have swirled around my feet as we talked. As Mother told me about the tree-trimming accident, I would have stared out my kitchen window at our own live oak that twisted up into the sky as if to throw a protective hand between the house and the sun. Perhaps Jay would have taken over, would have handled the packing of our bags, would have asked the neighbors to give our cat one scoop of dry food and a quarter can of wet every day. Perhaps he would have checked the oil in the car and made sure the tires were full of air. Maybe he would have said nice things about my father, or listened to whatever I had to say; I might have told him about the time Daddy'd been at the hospital so many nights in a row that Mother called him up and had him tell me a bedtime story over the phone. Mother listened on the kitchen phone and I listened in Mother and Daddy's bedroom, both of us in our night-gowns, the clamor of the emergency room behind Daddy's voice. The story was about a little girl who wanted to become an angel so a doctor put her to sleep and sewed wings onto her back.

"Where did he get the wings?" I asked.

"He . . . took them off another angel who had died," Daddy said.

"Fuuuuuck!" someone screamed in the background.

"Good night, Faith!" Daddy said.

"Good night," Mother and I said to each other; he was already gone.

When I let Richard into my room, he said, "I'm so sorry, Faith," and held his arms open to me. Walking into them, I felt as if I'd been trapped in a car with no brakes and had finally found something to stop me, some soft wall to crash against, like the walls in cartoons or in dreams. I held on to Richard as tightly as I could and cried into his neck about my father and everything else. "I bet he'll be okay," Richard said. Then he slid his face down the length of my face and kissed a slow line along my jawbone to my lips, and I pulled away. It wasn't an easy pulling, but I pulled all the same.

"Richard, I can't," I said.

"Why?" he said, his hands sliding from my waist.

"Because I'm married." I glanced at my wedding ring, as if to make sure.

"Because you'd rather be with a drunk," he said, backing away from me.

"No," I said. "I mean, yes. I mean, he's not going to be a drunk anymore."

"How do you know that, Faith?" Richard said. He'd

backed so far away from me that he was pressing up against my Thelonious Monk poster; Monk's torso seemed to grow directly out of Richard's head. "Is it because he *promised?*"

"I just know it," I said. "And when I don't know it, I hope it."

"Faith, hope, and love," he said, as he turned and opened the door and walked out. "Good fucking luck."

Formal Hedges

Daddy didn't die. He stayed in the hospital two days and Mother and I barely spoke over his hospital bed. I bought Texas-themed postcards at the hospital gift shop and sat in Daddy's room writing to Tonía. On the flip side of a photo of the globe with Texas expanded to cover most of it and the rest circled by a banner that read ON EARTH AS IT IS IN TEXAS, I wrote, "Dear Tonía, Isn't this card silly? I am at the hospital right now with my sick dad." I wanted to add that I was also there with my sick mother, but I refrained.

At the house, under the bed in the guest room, I found a box stuffed with Daddy's abandoned squares of knitting. I thought about trying to stitch them together into a blanket, trying to salvage something of them, but instead I closed up the box and shoved it back into the dust. I had a marriage to repair; I couldn't be fooling around with Daddy's stray squares of Mistake Stitch Ribbing.

At the house, Mother talked about relandscaping the front yard, as if Daddy had receded from her life to the point that she could go ahead and do whatever she wanted to the house, the yard, as if he wouldn't have the strength to object. "Are you sorry he's not going to die yet?" I asked her in a bad moment.

"Of course not," she said coolly, her mind on formal hedges, rose-covered gazebos.

I felt embarrassed over what I'd said because of this: Sometimes I wished Jay were dead. Sometimes my mind drifted off and suddenly I'd be imagining a phone call from the prison: Mrs. Evers? *Yes,* I would say stoically, knowing it was bad news. They'd tell me Jay had been killed in some vague prison incident, some fight with homemade knives fashioned from who knows what. Or, better yet, he had been trying to break up a fight between some other men, men with gangish nicknames like D-tron or Kooltrak. He had been his laid-back, sweet self, just stepping in to calm things down.

I wouldn't break down on the phone. I'd get all the necessary information about how to retrieve his body, then I'd call my mother and cry and cry. "Oh, Sugar," she'd say. She would sympathize while keeping her true opinion to herself: I'm better off without him.

I would wear a wonderful dress to the funeral, a black silk sheath and under it something naughty that Jay would have loved. Then things would gradually get better.

Men from the prison would write to tell me how Jay had inspired them in their own sobriety, how determined he was, how encouraging. Jay's counselor would send me the chips Jay had earned for his days of sobriety, and I would keep them in some pretty little box. Jay's mother would call me once a month and we'd weep over our shared memories of him. In direct contrast to reality, neither of us would blame the other for Jay's excesses. I would be incredibly grateful that he hadn't died of some sort of overdose. "My husband recently died of a massive heart attack," I would write to Tonía. "The girls and I miss him very much."

With the life insurance money I'd be able to buy another house, and with it a brand-new refrigerator, not one inch of which would be devoted to beer. After a while, I would have absolutely no idea of the price of marijuana, whether it was eighty dollars a quarter or five hundred. I would love being ignorant about such things. I would miss Jay's voice, body, eyes, the way he made up words and definitions in Scrabble and often got away with it ("Zoru, Buddy. You know, it's an ox with a big hump right behind its neck, native to India. You've seen it on one of those safari shows, little birds sitting on the hump pecking insects off the goddamn thing. I swear").

Choose one and only one of the following options: Faith is attracted to Jay because (a) she likes to feel superior, (b) she enjoys a challenge, (c) he's a hell of a Scrabble player, (d) all of the above, (e) none of the above.

Sometimes, right around the Scrabble part of my fantasy, I'd actually start crying. Then I'd reel my mind back in to the reality that Jay was perfectly alive, that what we had ahead of us would require far more effort than death. "Mo' effut than day-uth," I'd say to myself in a haughty southern accent. Sometimes I felt relieved, knowing I'd play Scrabble again with my husband, and sometimes it made me cry all the more.

Pork

Coach's idea about shortening the study lounge hours didn't result in any fattening of the team's win column; my boys racked up loss after loss. The embarrassed sportswriters who had picked us to do so well were moved to write one vicious article after another about Coach Walston. They questioned his ability to lead, his ability to call plays, his taste in clothes, his lack of facial expression on the sidelines. They ridiculed his wife's big hair, his reluctance to wear burnt orange, his disastrous statement to a reporter that he preferred pork barbeque to beef barbeque. The poor man was a native of Tennessee, after all, and apparently that's the kind of barbeque they eat there. But he should have known better than to say anything even vaguely anti-beef within the Texas state lines; he might as well have said he liked to slap babies.

When I saw Coach Walston in the halls of the athletic department, I wanted to hug him; I wanted to pat his sparsely covered head and tell him it was just a game. If Coach and I could have made everyone else in the world understand that it was just a game, everything would have been fine. Someone had to win, after all, and why not spread it around?

What did it matter whether it was the Longhorns or the Bears, the Aggies or the Sooners? But apparently it did matter, to quite a lot of people.

One dark day in early November, a week after Daddy came home from the hospital, my boys went out to their afternoon practice to find an effigy of Coach Walston hanging from one of the goalposts. They knew it was Coach because of the sign stuck to the figure's back that read I LIKE PIG! I could hardly get them to concentrate on their work that night, especially the younger ones who would still be in the program the next year. They had started to hear that dreaded word that pops up whenever a coach is about to be fired: *rebuilding. It's going to be a rebuilding year.*

"You shoulda seen it, Miss Evers," said Cam McClure. "It had eyeballs and everything, like real ones. Gary said they probably came offa cow."

"Maybe you could write about it," I said. Cam was on the verge of failing the yearlong creative writing class he had sworn to me would be easy.

"She said no horror stories," Cam said. "Someone tried to turn in a story about a vampire and she ripped it in half right in front of us."

"And it had, like, a buncha fake blood coming outta the mouth," Gary said.

"It's not Coach's fault we suck," said Cam.

"You guys are doing fine," I said. "It takes a long time to get good at something as complicated as football. Look at some of the professional teams. They get paid, first of all, and they don't have to go to classes and make their grades. They have all the time in the world to practice and some of them are still awful. I think, under the circumstances, that you guys are amazing. I'm very proud of you." *Rah, rah,* I thought.

"Coach is gonna get fired, isn't he?" Cam said.

"I hope not," I said, although I had just that day heard a rumor of a group of wealthy alums pooling their money to buy out the remaining year of Coach's contract, a tab of close to a million dollars. "Come on, everyone, let's get back to work. We don't need awful grades on top of a difficult season."

I couldn't get them calmed down enough to accomplish anything, so finally our study session degenerated into me letting them play Interview, a game in which they pretended to be professional athletes getting interviewed by reporters. My role, besides playing the reporter, was to keep them from sounding like bimbos. The day of the horrific loss to Texas Tech, I had just about fainted in front of the television when one of my linebackers told an ESPN reporter that "We just didn't got nothin' goin' on today on the offense or the defense, man."

"That first half was a tough one," I said to Gary Ecco, extending toward him my imaginary microphone, "but you really pulled it together in the third quarter. What happened at halftime that brought about such a dramatic change in the team's performance?"

"Yeah, uh, nothing happened really," Gary said. "Coach had a couple things to say but I think we just respond well to pressure and there's no pressure like going into the second half down by a couple touchdowns." He gave me one of his sweeter looks, the one that said *Is that right, teacher?*

"Let's revise that," I said. "You want to give your coach a little more credit, try not to start your sentences with 'yeah,' and make the whole statement a little more concise. Want to try again?"

"Coach made some excellent changes to our game plan during the half and we came out ready to respond to the pressure of being down by a couple of touchdowns and hopefully to win the game."

Everyone groaned.

"What?" Gary said.

"I am *hopeful* that we'll win the game. 'Perhaps we'll win the game,' the young quarterback said hopefully. Meaning he is full of hope. Remember? Have I not gone over this fifty thousand times already?"

"Yeah, okay. So I should have said, um, we came out ready to respond to being down by a couple of touchdowns and with hopes of winning the game."

"Much better, honey. Cam, you're next. What team?"

"Packers," he said, stroking the tattoo of a longhorn skull that covered his upper arm.

"All right, you cheesehead. Three turnovers in the first half put your team down by seventeen points. Could you talk about the effect of the turnovers on this game?"

"Well, we knew coming into this game that we'd have to avoid turning the ball over because we were up against a team that will capitalize on any mistake you make, and that's what they did today. Hi, Mom." He pressed the longhorn's eye sockets deeper into his arm.

"Good," I said. "I like the way you gave the other team credit for being wonderful instead of criticizing your own team for turning over the ball. You never want to put down your own teammates, and you did an excellent job of avoiding that."

"Thanks, Miss Evers."

I moved on to Mike Winston, who had mysteriously appeared in the football program in spite of having been suspended from baseball. "Mike, what team?"

"Don't care."

"Okay then, we'll make you a Cowboy."

"Raiders," he said.

Mike had shaved his goatee but had a new asymmetrical hairstyle that involved a thatch of hair that permanently obscured one eye. He glared at me with his blue, exposed eye as I said, "Mike Winston, you made the incredible forty-five-yard run that earned the winning touchdown for the Raiders. Tell us a little bit about the play and how it felt for you."

He tossed his head back, making sure to arrest the toss just before it would have disturbed the eye patch of hair, and said, "Just ran around them niggers, that's all."

"Get out," I said.

"Who's gonna make me?" he said. He leaned forward, almost revealing his hidden eye.

"I think some of your peers might be glad to help me, Michael, but I'm not going to put them in that position. You can either leave this room right now or I'll call security and have them escort you out. It's your choice."

He gathered his books as slowly as possible, picking up each item with a deliberate laziness that must have required far more concentration and strength than faster movements would have. I watched his slow, yogalike moves with hatred. I thought, *You are why I can't have my cat here, you big fucking baby.* I thought, *You don't know how close I am to breaking, you ignorant, illiterate little prick.* I summoned up horrible, condescending statements but didn't let them seep out of my mouth — just my eyes. I imagined Mike working a series of menial jobs, horrible jobs for which he would have to wear paper hats, hair nets, striped shirts. I was annoyed at myself for being so nice to him, for awarding him the hypothetical winning touchdown of some imaginary Raiders game. I was sorry I had nursed him through Intermediate French.

"See ya, Teach," he said as he swung the strap of his leather bag over his shoulder and started his arrogant, easy walk away from us. Every step he took sent a jolt of rage through me, a clean rage that crowded out everything else, even the words Richard Jamison had left on my answering machine earlier that day: "Faith, Richard here. I'd like to get together and talk and maybe before we do that you could do some thinking about the fact that your husband did sort of completely fuck up my life and don't you think you owe me something for that? I'm not talking about a civil trial, here, Faith, I'm talking about you returning a goddamn phone call, all right?" He spoke to me like an irritated sibling, like someone in a relationship so close that it can bear such talk, all the *fuck*s and *goddamn*s. Perhaps he got away with talking that way to Alice from time to time, in moments she ignored because they were cushioned by so many nicer ones, by him calling her sweet names and telling her she was the most wonderful woman in the whole wide world. And maybe Jay and I slipped into that sort of talk sometimes, sometimes when Jay would say, "Jesus fucking Christ, could I just have a goddamn drink without you looking at me like I'm the devil?" or when I would say, "Have your fucking drink! I hope you fucking drown in it!" Our marriages could put up with a certain measure of that, the way a soup can take a certain amount of salt and no more.

"Michael Winston," I called after him, "don't set foot in here again until you're ready to apologize to me and to your teammates."

"Sorry you're such a fucking bitch," he called over his shoulder as he walked out.

I knew I had asked the impossible of him, that it was not within the range of Mike's personality to apologize to me or anyone else. It seemed I was always asking the impossible, of myself and everyone around me. It was what Mother asked of her tomatoes, what the Longhorns fans asked of Coach Walston, what we all asked of each other. Some day, some strange and surprising day, I might just get it.

Now You Do

On the Friday night before the Texas A&M game, a week after Mike's tantrum, the entire first string, right down to the special teams and the born-again Christian contingent, got themselves sickeningly drunk. Apparently the prospect of losing to the Aggies was just too much for my boys, and they had decided to blot out the thought of it completely for a few hours.

The team stays together in an Austin hotel the night before home games, to prevent exactly this sort of thing from happening, but apparently maids were bribed and rooms were prestocked with hidden stashes of tequila. Harry, the defensive coordinator, came banging on my door at seven in the morning with the news that the offensive line was vomiting uncontrollably.

I held my robe tightly around me and said, "Harry, does this have something to do with their grades? I mean, I'm sorry about it, but why are you coming to me?"

"Faith, I know you're a very private person and I don't want to bring up a painful topic or anything, but back when your husband was on the radio, one of the guys heard him mention something about a hangover soup that you make, and we thought maybe you could just run over to the cafeteria and whip up a batch of it . . . please, Faith, we're all about to lose our jobs here. We need a win today and you know it. The press is out to crucify us. We've got the doctors on the way, but we need all the help we can get." Harry's hair had gone gray in the space of the season. It surprised me every time I saw him, even early in the morning, jolted from a dream of who knows what.

"Maybe I could just *run over* and *whip up* a batch of it?" I said.

"Well, that's what we were thinking. Please, Faith."

"Did Walston send you?"

"No," he said, "I thought of it myself," and I saw then how scared he was.

"I want the study lounge hours expanded back to the original schedule," I said.

"Sure, whatever you want."

"And Mike Winston can't have one drop of this soup until he apologizes to me and to the rest of the team for being a little racist brat the other day."

"Okay, we'll work on that."

"And I want you to promise me, right now, that you will never again call an athlete 'a fuckin' woman,' 'a girl,' 'a lady,' or anything else that's even slightly degrading to women. Ixnay on the exismsay, all right, Harry?"

"Okay, I promise."

"Do you think you can do it, Harry? I know it's a habit, and you'll have to try to break it. You'll have to think up some new way to humiliate them."

"Yeah, you know, I can do that."

I started to say, *And I want you to transform my husband into a law-abiding sober person, and while you're at it could you broaden my mother's attention span to include me?* I was tempted to reel off a list of wild, impossible demands: lunch on a gondola in Italy, a black forest cake rounded to the exact measurements of my left breast, a change of our national anthem to a more singable, accessible song. "Take Me Out to the Ball Game" perhaps.

Instead I said, "And why don't you just *run* out to the store and get me the ingredients I need while I take a shower."

"Okay, sure, just make me a list."

"Hold on," I said, and I found a piece of paper and started writing down the things I wanted. The recipe was lodged in my head, although I hadn't read it or made the soup in almost three years, although I had refused to divulge the ingredients to my very own husband and had sworn to him that he'd never eat my hangover soup again.

"Jesus, that's a lot of garlic," Harry said when he saw my list.

"Do you want the soup or not?"

"We owe you big, Faith. Okay, so, we've got a four P.M. kickoff. Do you think you could have it ready to go by, say, noon at the latest?"

"Sure." I considered giving him Jay's notebook, with its hundreds of cures, just letting him sort through the carefully transcribed stories like this one:

Hangover Cure #48, called in by a Robin who didn't want to give her last name but admitted it begins with the letter *E:* "Hi! Yeah, okay. Am I on? Oh, okay. Well, I like to drink as much as the next person, maybe a little more, and I tend to do really, well, sort of *stupid* things when I get drunk, although some people would probably say I do stupid things when I'm *not* drunk, but like the other night everything was going along fine and then suddenly I was dirty-dancing with my friend's boyfriend in our other friend's living room when we were all over there having dinner and we were gonna go out and hear some bands afterwards, and my boyfriend was there too but he's used to me, I guess, but now my friend is really pissed at me, like *really* pissed, like she gave me this big speech about *boundaries*, and she said I wouldn't recognize one if it jumped up and strangled me, and like she said pretty much everything I do is inappropriate — those were her two big words of the day, *boundaries* and *inappropriate* — and she was basically like, Why do you have to flirt with everyone else's boyfriend when you've got a perfectly good one of your own? So she was giving me this speech the next morning when I was really hung over, and my hangover kept getting worse and worse the more she talked, until finally the last time she said *inappropriate* I threw up right in front of her, and a little bit got on her shoes, actually, but then I felt a lot better. So maybe the thing to do is get one of your friends to lecture you about what an idiot you were the night before until you puke."

An hour later, Harry met me in the cafeteria with several bags of groceries. Maya sat on a stool, playing with the toys in her cornrows, probably a little offended that her own carefully devised, chock-full-o'-vitamins pregame meal had been scratched.

"I hear we got some hung-over student-athletes," she said, stretching the foolishness of *student-athletes* like state fair taffy.

"Not for long," Harry said, cheerfully dumping out one of the bags to create a mountain of garlic on the stainless steel counter. Maya grabbed his burnt orange shirttail as he tried to pass her to leave.

"Not so fast," she said. "This young lady and I ain't peeling all that garlic by ourselves."

"Uh, I got pregame meetings," Harry said. "I'll send one of my assistants over, how's that?"

"We need you now, Harry," I said. "Just tell Coach it was all my fault. Tell him I was being an unreasonable premenstrual bitch."

"Oh I wouldn't do that . . ." Harry trailed off. He grabbed a pile of garlic and a cutting board, probably hoping that a frantic show of labor would keep me from saying anything else about my menses.

We peeled and chopped and squeezed. Our fingers grew sticky with garlic.

"Isn't there some other way?" Harry said after the mountain had shrunk only a little.

"What do you mean?"

"Like a machine or something."

"It has to be hand-peeled, Harry. The enzymes in human skin react with the garlic in a way that enhances its hangover-curing properties," I lied.

"Oh, okay," Harry said. "I didn't know that. You know, my wife buys these little jars of garlic, already mashed up. You just use it straight from the jar."

"That's not garlic, Harry," I said. "Don't even call that garlic."

"Okay, okay."

"Hey, Harry, you gonna know a lot about garlic after today, no?" Maya said. "Not so much about football."

"Yeah, well, speaking of football . . ."

"Go check on my poor hung-over babies," I said. "Tell them they're in for a treat."

"Thanks, Faith," Harry said, whipping off his apron. "See you at noon."

Maya and I laughed when we were sure he was gone. "You got some work out of him," Maya said.

"Not as much as he's getting out of me."

Then we quieted down and started to work in earnest. I told Maya how to do the vegetable stock for the soup; although it felt strange to give instructions to someone with so much cooking experience, I just did it and told myself that I probably had more experience with hung-over husbands than she did.

Choose one and only one of the following options: Faith is attracted to Jay because (a) he's such a fuck-up that she feels highly competent in comparison, (b) he's gorgeous, (c) the sum of a bunch of tenuous things such as Jay planting a crate of tulip bulbs in the backyard one fall and Faith thinking when the hell did Jay get interested in tulips, watching him through the window as he knelt in the yard with a beer in one hand and the pearly bulbs in the other, and then the next spring the flowers came up and spelled out her name in huge capital letters, a bunch of things like this that add up to love, (d) all of the above, (e) none of the above.

We cracked the fragile eggs, smashed the sturdy garlic, ground up the hard black peppercorns, and at last we had a giant pot of hangover soup.

"There's one more thing," I said to Maya.

"What's that?"

"We both have to spit in it."

She touched a hand to my forehead, as if to say, *Girl, have you lost it?* Then she said, "The enzymes in spit react with the garlic in a special way?"

"No," I said. "It's just their punishment for getting so fucking drunk."

Maya opened her mouth and laughed so hard that a little preliminary spit flew into the pot. "One, two, three," she said, and we both did it. It made me feel wonderful, just like always.

Early in the afternoon, when my damaged ballplayers filed into the cafeteria, I saw in each one of them an incarnation of Jay. Cam McClure, in particular, had turned his skin a very pale grayish green, a color that might, in some clothing catalog, be called sea foam, or celery. Some of them seemed thinner, with more definition than usual between their heads and their necks, while some seemed bloated, with tiny, poisonous pillows swelling beneath their eyes. They walked as if their skins were the wrong sizes for their skeletons. They moved gingerly, quietly, wary of noise. I always hated that part about Jay's hangovers; I knew he wasn't himself when he didn't want to listen to music. On those days I tended to get a sudden urge to listen to something myself: some complicated, exhausting jazz, some pounding, triumphant opera. "Please, Buddy," Jay would whisper from beneath his pillow.

Please, Jay! I felt like yelling back. Our hangovers were inverted; I experienced mine while he was actually drunk, my veins filling up with dread and sadness and the desire to be cleansed.

I didn't really need to be in the cafeteria; Maya had her regular servers there to ladle out the soup. But I wanted to watch my boys sweat as the soup started to do its work on them. I wanted to watch them clutch their muscular foreheads as they felt the garlic's first sting. I wanted to give them one of my classic pep talks if their courage began to fail them. Or I thought I did, anyway. It turned out that as I watched their faces glow with sweat, as I saw them reach for paper napkins to stop their suddenly active sinuses, I felt the urgent need to cry, realizing I'd seen this all before. I stood behind the serving counter, scanning the line of boys to see if it included Mike Winston, until Harry came up and told me that Mike had said he'd rather be hung over forever than apologize to me.

"He needs an attitude transplant," I said.

"Faith, you probably know the kid better than we do. He's got more talent than God but no motivation. Walston thinks if we push him too hard he'll just quit the program."

"He's out of my program, Harry. I told him not to come back until he was ready to apologize."

"Well, that's between you and Coach, I guess."

"I guess." Then I thanked Maya for her help and walked toward the door.

"Miss Evers," Cam groaned as I passed.

"What?" I said. Even the horns on his longhorn tattoo seemed to droop.

"It hurts," he said.

"I know it does," I said, and I walked outside.

I had felt so strong and superior, cooking up my hangover soup. Stripping naked all that garlic, I'd felt happy that my husband wasn't the only person in the world who gets stinking drunk. But outside, my back pressed up against the dirty bricks of the cafeteria, I felt the most awful part of me, the part I kept shriveled to a kernel, swell up and expand to fill my whole self. I hadn't quite realized, the night I threw myself down on Heinz Fechtler's bed, that I had a whole lifetime to live out on the other side of that night. It had made me careful, the way that night burned and glowed and refused to die out. I walked through my days as carefully as my hungover student-athletes had eased their way into the cafeteria.

I'm trying to think now how things were between Jay and me on that day, the day of the Longhorns-A&M game. How things were between us at any given moment depended mostly on the last letter either one of us had received from the other, or sometimes on our last visit. But often even a wonderful letter from Jay was diluted by the fact that I knew, on reading it, that the feelings expressed there had been felt several days before, that Jay had moved on and was perhaps, at the very moment that I read his declarations of love, writing angry bits of things in the margins of his notebook during a sobriety class, his handwriting gone jagged, or maybe he was sitting in a group meeting spilling the horrific details of our marriage. I know we were past the first phase of his imprisonment, the phase during which we were both proud of the fact that Jay had turned himself in. I'm pretty sure we were already into the bitter, boring phase, when time stretched out ahead of us like a dull and endless

West Texas road. Even our letters had grown stale; Jay had run out of things to tell me about his narrow little world, and I felt guilty describing to him the nice parts of mine: the warm fall days, Lucy's new sound that vaguely resembled my name, the strange satisfaction I got at the Recording for the Blind studio when I intentionally changed some fact in a textbook, when I increased the number of Alamo survivors or included chocolate in their list of provisions, when I was able to rewrite history.

As I walked back up to my dorm room, not sure what I would do with myself until game time, I tried to think of something I could write to Jay. Writing to Tonía was so easy; I spent most of my letters to her describing my imaginary children, what good girls they were, how proud of them I was. I began composing a letter to Tonía in my head: *My daughter Ellen is developing quite a talent for softball. She is the pitcher for her team, the Pandas, and she throws with an accuracy and speed unusual for her age. Even though the pitches are thrown underhand, I worry that so much throwing will affect her arm somehow. My husband tells me not to worry, and just to keep cheering.*

I was so engrossed in my vision of my softball-playing daughter and the potential damage to her little rotator cuff that I didn't even see Richard standing in my doorway until I almost ran into him, one hand buried in my bag in search of my keys.

"A peso for your thoughts," Richard said.

"A whole peso?" I said, taking a step back, and then another, wondering how he had made it past security. "Usually I get only a penny."

"You look amazing," he said. "I thought I'd be able to guess your entrance code. Your drunk husband's birthdate."

"How did you know it?"

"There's this thing called the Internet. You look great."

"You don't look so well, Richard," I said. "You look tired." And he did; his beard was uneven, his eyes two broken places.

"Why haven't you returned my calls?" he said.

"Because I'm married, Richard."

"Still married to the drunk." He edged toward me.

"I'm still married to Jay, yes." I didn't back up; it seemed important to stand my ground.

"You know," he said, "Alice's face was so fucked up we couldn't even have her casket open at the funeral. They couldn't make her look anything like who she was."

"I didn't know that," I said.

I started to say something about my grandmother, who had died a few years before, about how she hadn't looked at all like herself in her coffin, about how tired I'd grown of people at the funeral saying, "She looks so beautiful." *Except that she's dead*, I had wanted to say back. But in the middle of my thought, Richard pulled his fist from the pocket of his coat and swung it across the left side of my face. I heard my glasses hit the wall on the other side of the hallway, felt my bag swing to the floor. I heard Richard say, "Now you do," as he hit me again. I opened my mouth to scream, but Richard closed it with his fist. *Now you do.* He grabbed my shoulder to steady me, then hit me so hard I slammed back against the wall, felt my jaw come unhinged. I couldn't seem to keep my eyes open, my feet flat on the floor. I tried to cover my head, my face. I smelled the garlic on my fingers as I tried to bring them up to my face, smelled it just for an instant before my nose filled with blood. Richard wouldn't let me fall; he pinned me to the wall with a knee against my pelvis; he pulled back his fist and hit me again and again. I had the idea that we probably looked sort of funny, and awkward, that his punches weren't graceful and well-delivered like the ones you see in movies, that I made a floppy, uninteresting victim, stupid with surprise.

He hit me a few times in the gut, in the space between my breasts, but he always remembered my face and came back to it. He drew noises from me I had never heard before, little breathy surprises. He said, "Now you do," as often as he could gather his breath to say it, and I forgot what he was talking about. I forgot about everything: Jay, football, tomatoes, the way Leo Rhodes had stolen home in a completely unimportant game in the last week of the season, a game that took place after victory would no longer help us, how we all jumped up and down anyway. The hallway was so quiet, but I couldn't remember why; I forgot that everyone was at the cafeteria eating my hangover soup. *Now you do.* I grew dumber with each punch, with each softening of my face, until I was so stupid I thought surely Jay must be on his way, that any minute he'd be there to help me, then I couldn't remember even Jay. I wanted to scream just to fill up the world with noise, just to let out some of the fire in my face, but I couldn't get a breath. *Now you do.* My brain felt slushy in my skull. I tried to solidify it, to keep it from melting; I tried to make it hold its shape long enough for me to fill my lungs with air and scream. *Now you do.* I heard a door opening, footsteps, another wet landing on my cheek, then someone pulled Richard off me and I fell into the space that had been Richard's knee.

"Hold on, Miss Evers," someone called, the voice receding, then a grinding thud and something slammed against the wall beyond and above me, again and again, and I knew then that the voice was Mike Winston's.

"Hold on, okay?" he yelled.

Mike's voice, full of air, had been yanked up from its usual sullen register; something was happening that interested him. This was more interesting than the game, than his own head-crushing hangover, than any class he would ever take. I almost wanted to teach him something while the door to his mind swung tantalizingly open. But I was tired, burning, using all my strength to keep my face from touching the floor; I sensed that it would hurt very much if I let my face touch anything.

"Fucker!" Mike yelled, and I heard a final, sloppy thud. Then a lumbering, slow thing dragged past me, but I couldn't turn my head to look; instead I watched the fire-black insides of my eyelids. After I don't know how long, Mike ran back past me, calling, "Just a sec, Miss Evers!" Then his big feet were near my head and it didn't matter that my eyes were already swollen shut; I knew his complicated shoes by heart.

"Security's gonna take care of him, Miss Evers," he said, and he picked me up in his arms without so much as a groan and he carried me out to his car, his horrible little sports car with the Confederate flag sticker on one side of the bumper and the YOU WEAR YOUR X AND I'LL WEAR MINE sticker on the other side, and he drove me to the hospital. It was just like Mike, I thought, heavy in his arms, not to have the patience to wait for an ambulance. He was that way in every sport; he'd make the play himself because he couldn't bear to wait for his teammates to do it.

The radio was on in Mike's car, some pregame speculation about whether Coach Walston would lose his job if my boys were defeated by the Aggies that afternoon, or even if they weren't; my pulse ached to the beat of it. I kept thinking my face had been burned; I kept thinking there had been fire in Richard's hands.

"It's okay, Miss Evers," Mike said in his new voice. "I think I broke his nose. I'm pretty sure I at least busted his nose," and then I understood that Mike had probably made a pudding out of Richard's face and that he had done it not only because he was a hot-tempered southern boy but because it was his way of apologizing to me. "Don't you worry about anything, Miss Evers," he said. "They'll fix you up. They can fix anything now, you know? Hey, I heard from Micah last night. Called to wish me luck in the game or somethin'. I told him we're gonna get our butts kicked."

I tried to say, *No, no you are not going to get your butts kicked and what kind of attitude is that, Michael Winston! How are you ever going to win the Game of Life with that sort of attitude?* But my lips were too thick to let the words out; *attitude* possessed an impossible number of syllables that knocked against my gums and shot pains through my teeth and then flattened against my tongue. I tried one more time, thinking if I used enough breath I could force the words out.

The last thing I remember was pushing, gathering a force from the center of my chest and hoping it would follow the course I imagined for it, but the next time I woke up I was in a hospital bed, in the dark, between sheets that seemed to have been chilled to the perfect temperature for someone with fire in her face, for someone like me.

I'm Not Married to Harry

In the third summer of our marriage, KXAL had sent Jay to a convention of disc jockeys in Chicago and I went along with him. One afternoon Jay skipped a seminar called "Who Is Your Audience?" and we sat in the bleachers at Wrigley Field and watched the Cubs get crushed by the Reds. The Cubs were our favorite National League team, and normally we would have been very interested in the outcome of the game, but being in Wrigley changed all that. The ballpark was so beautiful, with its ivy-covered walls and the sun making the bricks look almost soft, that once we were in there, we didn't care who won or lost. We were happy just to be present.

Harry Caray, the wonderful old Cubs announcer, was still alive then, and we stood with him during the seventh-inning stretch as he led the crowd in singing a raucous, off-key version of "Take Me Out to the Ball Game." He swayed, leaning out of the announcer's booth, threatening to fall out. I waved as if he could see me. I was thrilled to see Harry in person, having sung with him over the radio and television many times.

"You love Harry," Jay said as we settled back into our seats. "And he's a drunk. A notorious drunk."

"I'm not married to Harry," I said.

Other drunks Jay held up as examples were William Faulkner, Hank Williams, and Noah.

"The people who'll tell you Noah wasn't a drunk," Jay said to me once, "are the same people who think Song of Solomon isn't about sex." Jay didn't know much about the Bible, but he could, in the resounding voice of a preacher, quote the verse about Noah being drunk and naked.

Waking up in the hospital before dawn the morning after Richard had broken my face, I imagined I had a choice: Jay biblically drunk and naked, or no Jay. Then I remembered it was a choice I had already made once, one that had led me to where I was right then. If I had not walked out of our house that spring morning, had not driven to campus and installed myself in the dorm, what would have happened to Jay? Most likely he would have gone on drinking and I would have continued with my nagging. But Alice Jamison wouldn't have died. I wouldn't have met Richard. Maybe, just maybe, Jay would have grown out of his habit.

I told myself, in Gisela's commanding German accent, to stop it. I had done my best, although my best was only a human best. I had done my best. Still, I badly needed to hear my mother say, "Sugar, it all comes out in the wash." I imagined she would be there soon, looming over my bedside with the scent of soil on her hands, and I tried to sleep until her voice would wake me.

We Lost That Game, Miss Evers

One day when I sat in on the creative writing class that almost broke Cam McClure, the T.A. lectured about things she did not want to see in her students' assignments, things that were, as she said, "Cop-outs, okay?"

She made it clear, through repeated use of the words *pet peeve* and *lame*, that the students were not allowed to use photographs in their fiction to demonstrate the relationship between two people: No "I slowly pick up the photograph of Jay and me on our wedding day, me with my hair in a perfect French twist and Jay with a glass of champagne in each hand and another balanced on his head." They were not allowed to use dreams for any reason, but especially not as a parallel to something in a character's life. No "In my dream the fog formed thick, vertical columns, too narrowly spaced for me to run through. I could see Jay on the other side, relaxing on an inflatable raft in a sparkling pool of Budweiser, but the bars of fog grew thicker, and thicker." They were also strictly forbidden to write stories about college students in Prague. "If I have to read one more Prague story," the T.A. said from behind her tiny eyeglasses with the almond-shape lenses, "I will freak."

In spite of having received such instruction and having carefully edited Cam's efforts for dreams, photos, and Prague, I spent nearly all of my first few days in the hospital dreaming crazy dreams, summoning up photographs of my life from behind my swollen-shut eyes. It was all I had to do besides listen to the voices of my visitors: Mother, Darrah, and the kind Officer Shane, who informed me that his mother had taught him early on that "shouldn't no one hit a woman." Officer Shane made me perversely want to pry my eyes open to have a look-see. He made me want to shout, "Shane! Shane!" in a pitiful, cinematic voice. Officer Shane informed me that a message had been sent to my husband about my "condition." Although I couldn't see his face, I could tell from his voice that he thought my life was an awful mess. He told me that Richard Jamison was still in custody, that he had a "fancy-ass" lawyer and was about to undergo a psychiatric evaluation. Officer Shane speculated that Richard thought he could weasel out of his assault charges by claiming some type of temporary insanity brought on by the death of his wife. It was clear that Officer Shane thought even the death of a wife was a pitiful excuse for hittin' a woman.

Darrah explained to me in her most informed, motherly tones that she thought it would be upsetting to Lucy to see my, you know, face, but she brought me a recording of the baby's voice making all kinds of loose vowel sounds in between Darrah and Daniel's prompting to "Say *Faith*. Come on, Lucy, say hi to Aunt Faith." Lucy's wandering little opera started to pull together the beginnings of a laugh that cranked up the pain in my abdomen just a notch before I intentionally thought of something not funny to stop it. My unfunny thought was *I wonder what we should do about our taxes this year.*

Coach Talwen came to see me with a card signed by all the returning baseball players. He read it to me in a stilted, embarrassed voice. Cory Bell's portion of the card included a Bible verse and what Coach described as a small drawing of a cross with several light rays emanating from it. The gist of the verse was that I had some heavy-duty rewards piling up in Heaven due to my recent suffering. That sounded good to me. "Faith," Coach said, "I don't want you to worry about your job, now. Seems like you already had everyone pretty well ready for finals, and your staff's agreed to pitch in, and thank God we've got Christmas break coming up here. Who knows, you might be up and going by the start of the semester. Get those boys started off right. I think we've got a chance this year. Course, you never know, but it's not out of the question."

Mike Winston came and held my hand and said, "Miss Evers, you know that thing that happened before Mic took off? When I kicked Bell in the ribs and all? I'm sorry I did that. You tried to stop me and I did it anyway and I'm real sorry, Miss Evers." *Is this a dream?* I wondered. *Am I going to be penalized for this in creative writing class?* "And, Miss Evers," he said, his apology mechanism well lubricated now, the words flowing quickly and sorrowfully, "you know when I said that thing about the black guys on your imaginary team? That was bad, Miss Evers. I don't know why I did that, either, and I'm real sorry. I know better than to talk like that. I just said it for the hell of it, and I wish I hadn't. I'm gonna take those stickers off my car, too, Miss Evers. Next time I go to the car wash, I promise you. And you know what, Miss Evers? I was just gettin' outta the shower when I heard that stuff happening to you and when I punched that guy my towel kinda fell off. I hope you didn't see nothin'."

If I could have talked I would have said, "Anything, honey. I can't see anything without my glasses."

Mike patted my hand as he talked, and my hand felt tiny between his two large ones. He patted more and more enthusiastically, and I thought of Jay yanking on our rosemary plant, of my saying, "Don't yank, Jay, just pet it gently."

"And you know what, Miss Evers? There were a couple of guys on the hall that day, some fucking little chem major and this faggy little mechanical engineer. I gave 'em hell for not comin' out and helping you, Miss Evers. They said they heard somethin', but they thought it was just two football players beatin' on each other. I'm gonna get them, Miss Evers, if I can figure out how without gettin' myself in trouble, you know."

No, no, no! I wanted to say.

"We lost that game, Miss Evers," Mike said. "To the Aggies. They smeared us all over the field. I was kinda wishing my eyes were swollen shut like yours, when I read what they wrote about us in the Sunday paper. They had this massive picture of Coach and a headline with the letters about as tall as a building saying 'UT's Darkest Hour.' I don't see why that was our darkest hour. Isn't that what you call a, whatchamacallit, a simile?"

I longed to break loose from the wires in my jaw, to say *hyperbole.*

Two of my spunkier Meals on Wheels patients took a cab to the hospital to visit me: Mrs. Kelsey and Mr. Kinney. They were in the program only because their arthritis made it difficult for them to prepare food for themselves; even operating a can opener was beyond them.

Their small gasps and tongue-cluckings when they first saw me were quickly covered with jokes about the food, about how I was getting a taste of my own medicine with this food meant only for the sick and the dead, now wasn't I, and isn't this a lovely room, last time the two of them had been in a hospital, Mrs. Kelsey with her kidneys and Mr. Kinney because he'd gotten down in the back, they'd had the gloomiest rooms you'd ever hope to see, it would make a person sick just to set one toe in there.

They talked more to each other than to me, which was understandable because at least they could goad responses out of each other, whereas my jaw was locked shut and my eyelids still too heavy to open, my brain sodden with dreams and out-of-focus photographs. If I could have spoken, I would have begged them for a radio. I would have had them turn the dial until I was sure Jay's voice was nowhere to be found.

They didn't stay long; they had about five other rooms to hit while they were there. *When you get to be our age, Faith, honey, all you do is haul your old bones back and forth between the cemetery and the hospital.*

And Mother. Mother said one wonderful thing after another, vague, homey things that made me feel better. *Everything will be okay, honey. Sugar, this will all come out in the wash.*

Sometimes, when I was sleepy and medicated and the dark behind my eyelids was shot through with silvery threads, I thought, *Maybe Jay will be here later.* Slightly more alert, I'd pry that thought from my mind, I would toss it aside and call up the image of Cam McClure's creative writing teaching assistant, her hair of a dark red, almost gory color, her strict list of don'ts, and I'd make up my own: Don't expect Jay. Don't even imagine the taste of solid food because it's going to be weeks. Don't go nuts because three years of work with Mike Winston hasn't changed him into a man who knows a simile when he hears one. Don't give in to your mother's offer to open your letters from Jay and read them to you; keep something between you and your husband if it's the last thing you do. Don't waste your energy making grunts of protest when the nurses mistakenly refer to you as a victim of domestic violence; don't even try to tell them that you haven't been the least bit domestic in months, that your last attempt at domesticity was concocting a giant pot of hangover soup that didn't even bring your team a victory. Don't forget that you are a very sick girl.

Vacation

My first four days in the hospital, with my eyes and my mouth sealed up from the outside world, I had plenty of time to think. I didn't spend it the way I often did, concocting schemes to help my student-athletes avoid utter and humiliating failure. I didn't think about the composition of the Earth's crust, about how to wrest a page of Prague-free fiction from Cam, about Spanish verbs or Victorian poetry. I didn't think about Macbeth and his wife, about Gary Ecco's idea that Lady Macbeth must have been "a great lay" in order to convince her husband to commit murder. I didn't think about the physics of baseball, about the difference between a curveball and a breaking ball and whether our Micah-less pitching staff had hopes of throwing either one with any success the next spring. I didn't think about torn rotator cuffs and anterior cruciate ligaments, about the terrible crunching noises my football players made when they tackled each other during practice. I didn't even think about Richard, about how the man who had cheered for the Cubs with me had become someone who smashed my face in. I didn't think about Tonía, about all the lies I had written to her, about the world she thought I inhabited, the one with the dentist husband and three beautiful little girls, the world in which I ferried gorgeous, razor-smart children from soccer practice to birthday parties to violin rehearsal. I didn't think about Mother's garden, about how her fall vegetables must be rotting on their vines while she sat in my hospital room watching my face change color and saying one loving thing after another, starting all her sentences with "Sugar." I didn't think about Alice Jamison and the men we had married, how they could both be so wonderful or awful. I didn't think about why I had survived Alice's husband while she had not survived mine. I thought about me.

Apart from knocking loose two of my permanent teeth, apart from breaking my jaw and my nose and making such a mess of my face that Darrah had to keep it from Lucy the way she would protect her from knowledge of monsters under the bed and bogeymen, Richard had knocked loose something in my heart. I was suddenly tired of fixing things: term papers, the soufflé-like egos of my athletes, my marriage. I was tired of figuring out how to make things work, tired of rigging up weird solutions to problems I hadn't caused in the first place. I was exhausted from blaming myself for Alice Jamison's death. Jay could have done a hundred things in response to my night with Heinz — he could have ranted, wept, prayed — instead of operating a motor vehicle blind-drunk. I was tired of living in a dorm. I was sick of dreading my thirtieth birthday. I was tired of thinking about Jay.

I'm not sure I can explain why what Richard did made me so damn tired, tired not only in my physical body but in my heart as well. Maybe it's that Richard used up the last of my energy so I no longer had anything left for Jay. Perhaps his punches rearranged things in my brain, shook everything up so that my thoughts were left in a different order. Maybe knowing that I hadn't deserved to be hit that way led me to the knowledge that I hadn't deserved all that drunkenness. I wish I had a better explanation, but I don't. I'm sorry.

The first day I was able to open my eyes, when everything seemed so bright that Mother had to keep the shades tightly closed and the lights in my room turned off, I entertained Darrah with sign language until she understood that I wanted a pen and a piece of paper.

"I love you," I wrote on it first.

"I love you, too," she said, her eyes bright with tears.

"If I write something to J. will you mail it to him w/out reading it?" I wrote.

"Sure," she said. "Of course."

"Will you bring me a picture of Lucy?"

"Yeah," she said. "I've got some new ones." Darrah's hair had grown out almost to her chin; it made me feel that a great deal of time had passed.

Later that night, when Darrah and Mother had left, I wrote Jay a letter. I told him, among other things, that I needed a vacation from him. I told him I would keep my promise, that I would wait for him, but that I wouldn't be able to write or visit for a while. I struggled to find a word that sounded less frivolous than *vacation,* then gave up and wrote *vacation.* I folded the letter into a tight, tiny square, and shoved it under my pillow.

I still hadn't seen the face of the woman who was taking a vacation from her husband. Darrah had claimed not to have a mirror in her purse when she visited, and Mother had taped a grocery bag over the bathroom mirror with the message "You Are Beautiful, Faith Anne" written on it in red marker. I shoved off my covers and went into the bathroom and pulled aside the bag. I opened my eyes wide and turned on the light.

Well, I could get into a long, whiny description of my face here. I could make extended comparisons to overripe eggplant, to roadkill simmering by the highway on a hot summer day. I could recall certain monsters from certain horror movies. Swamp creatures. Bubbly, yeasty lab experiments gone awry. But suffice it to say that I carefully taped Mother's bag back over the mirror and read her message several times. Her handwriting was beautiful, her words even more so. They started to twist and glow, to reach out to me with a feverish, liquid urgency. I watched *Faith Anne* grow dim and then brighten, the letters blurring bravely into each other and then shrinking back into themselves. I gripped the edge of the sink, trying to squeeze hard enough to make Mother's words stand still. The grocery bag grew more and more textured, revealing deep, scoured, glacial valleys like the ones Micah and I had learned about in History of the Earth. Then Mother's words faded into the bag's mountainous landscape, and without them I badly wanted to be back in my bed. I used the sink as a shoving-off place and stumbled back in the direction of the bed and tried to fall against the button that would bring a nurse, and I met the floor not knowing if I had reached my goal or not.

Dream Garden

I spent almost five weeks in the hospital, due to what the doctors called a subdural hematoma, which, as I understand it, means Richard hit my head so hard that my brain bled. Actually, it wasn't my brain that bled but a vein on top of it. I know this medical vagueness on my part would drive my father the doctor nuts, but I get a kick out of saying "my brain bled." I like to imagine my brain bleeding the way a cloud squeezes out rain, leaving me lighter, cleaner, less troubled.

Mother complained that they should have scanned my brain right away, instead of waiting until I collapsed in my room; she told the doctors, "I was married to Henry all the way through med school and believe me, I know a thing or two about medicine."

"Claire, let the doctor do his job," said Daddy, who had rushed over from Houston after my collapse. He sat in my room knitting a big green blob, afraid the time off from work would leave his hands stiff and incapable.

"Make me something, Daddy," I scribbled on a notepad, unable to talk around the breathing tube in my mouth.

"I don't know how, Faith," he said. "But I'll try."

Dr. Langley, my neurosurgeon, who ignored Mother's criticisms and called her "Claire" while he called Daddy "Dr. Abbott," had to suction out my brain blood by drilling three holes in my skull and cutting out a circle of bone above my left ear. I was hoping he would suction out a few other things, while he was at it: the thousands of versions of Jay's face, his face smiling and in motion with thought after thought the way the sky is sometimes in motion with wind; Jay's face brick-still and heavy with gin; Jay's face lined with the many gutted, dusty inroads of our marriage; Jay's face happy and alive, his mouth taking shape to call me "Buddy"; Jay's face.

Mother stayed with me the whole time, while I grew sicker and sicker. It seems that my collapse in front of the mirror was actually a seizure, during which I *puked*, as one of Jay's callers might say, and sucked the *puke* back into my lungs. Please excuse the revolting details; I don't really know how else to explain the way I developed aspiration pneumonia and then something the nurses called ARDS, or acute respiratory distress syndrome. *Acute* and *distress* were my favorite words of the four. They described perfectly the state of my life, both outside the hospital and in it, and I wished the doctors and nurses would say them, the whole words, instead of using the abbreviation. The abbreviation was worth it only when Mother said it, usually on the phone with her friends, or with Daddy when he went back to work, because of the way she said *S: A-yuhs.*

I had plenty of time to analyze Mother's lovely southern accent because she never left my side, including Christmas morning when she probably would have liked to be home with Daddy. He had to work; the hospital is apparently a

popular place on Christmas Day, with kids slicing themselves to pieces on their new toys and drunk people hurting
each other. In my own hospital room, Mother did what she
usually spent the winter days doing — reading seed catalogs
and gardening books — only she read them aloud to me.

"Oh, this sounds like a good one," she said on Christmas.
"Listen, Sugar: it's called Oregon Spring Bush Tomato. It
says here, 'Luscious red, slightly flattened globes are sweet
and juicy, producing two to four fruits per pound. Produces
well when nights are cool.' Oh, well, never mind about that
one. Let's see if I can find one that produces well when
nights are so scorching hot you'd like to die."

Santa Claus is coming to town was being piped in from
somewhere, perhaps from my own bloody brain.

"Now *here's* a good one," Mother said. "It's called a Thes-
saloniki, or however you say that. It's a Greek variety —
now I think that's good, because Greece is pretty damn hot,
or at least it was the time your father and I went — I remember saying to Henry that we could have just stayed in Texas
to be hot instead of doing it in a whole new country. Anyway it says, 'Firm, juicy, incredibly flavorful, resistant to
cracking.' I think I'll try that one." I heard her fold down the
corner of the catalog's page. I could imagine the pleased expression on her face as she envisioned the rows and rows of
firm and juicy Greek tomatoes she'd have by next summer. I
stared at the textured ceiling that looked like dried cottage
cheese and I drifted into a medicated fantasy about the day I
would be over my ARDA-*yuhs* and would be able to breathe
on my own, without the breathing tube that kept me silent
and the sedatives that kept me relatively still. Occasionally
Mother got up from her chair and walked over to hold a page

of the catalog a few inches in front of my face, as she did now with the Greek tomato. "Doesn't it look promising, honey?" she said. The page was a blur of round, red shapes.

I guess so, I mouthed silently around the breathing tube while Mother stared very hard at my lips. Mother loved lip-reading; she could pretend I was saying whatever she wanted to hear.

"I'm glad you think so," she said. "I knew you'd like that one."

I'll have a blue Christmas without you . . .

"You know something, Sugar," Mother said, back in her chair, "I think a garden would do you worlds of good. If you ever get into a house with a yard, that is. Or you might see if the university doesn't have some kind of community plot where you could grow a few things. I just hate to see you pouring yourself into these things — your athletes, and Jay, of course — and getting nothing back. A garden gives back every bit of what you put into it and more, honey. I couldn't have stood the last thirty-five years without my garden, I'll tell you that. Oh, here's a nice one. Listen to this, Sugar. This one's called Orange Oxheart and they say it's a bright orange-yellow, very meaty with a hearty flavor. 'One bite of an Orange Oxheart and you'll think you've gone to heaven,' they say here. Well, that's quite a recommendation, wouldn't you say?"

I would say that Mother and I were having some of the best conversations of our lives. I would say she had risen to the occasion with me the way she did with her garden when it was afflicted by an insect invasion. She had thought up a way to mother me just as she had thought up the perfect solution to the tomato beetles that had plagued her garden one summer: sucking them off the plants with a Dustbuster.

"Now what about this one, Sugar? It's called Doublerich, and they claim it has twice the vitamin C content of any other tomato. Well, I don't know if that's exactly what I'm looking for in a tomato. Also, it's bred in North Dakota. The poor things would probably have fits down here."

Mother didn't even need the catalog seeds; she had plenty of seeds of her own, saved from her garden over the years and some passed down from my grandmother. But she loved to try new things. She loved to come across some new variety in a catalog and believe every word they wrote about it.

Probably, I mouthed, although she wasn't looking.

Something something figgy pudding, and a happy New Year!

I wanted to ask Mother if she'd ever grown figs, if she knew how to make a figgy pudding. But I just listened, and formed my mouth into the shape of a word every once in a while, and at night I dreamed of tomato vines unlatching the circle in my skull and twisting into my brain, soaking up the blood with their furry green stalks. Mother read to me day after day, through New Year's Eve and through my thirtieth birthday on the seventh of January, when she read me the recipe for the hazelnut chocolate cake she promised to bake for me whenever I was well enough to eat cake. I cried when she read "Eight ounces unsweetened chocolate," it sounded so good. She told all the nurses it was my birthday and suggested they pipe something delicious in through that tube in my nose.

But mostly she read to me from seed catalogs, made lists of

the seeds she wanted to order, cut out pictures of the ripe vegetables and pasted them on a big piece of posterboard and declared it her dream garden. As the dream garden evolved into a paradise of pathways, arches and tomato vines trained in obese shapes against a cool stone wall, the nurses gradually weaned me off the ventilator and I learned to breathe on my own again. My favorite was Nurse Weaver, who admonished my lazy lungs in her West Texas drawl, "This thing's doing ninety percent of the work for you, honey babes. I bet tomorrow the doctors will take it down to eighty percent or so, and pretty soon this free ride will be over, you hear?"

"She's going to hit you with a ruler if you don't shape up," Mother said from her corner.

I loved the way Nurse Weaver wore hideous eyeglasses, blue plastic frames shot through with streaks of yellowish brown. I loved the way she called my lungs "honey babes," staring at my chest as she spoke, as if she had X-ray vision and could see clearly their slothfulness. I would have liked to put a few of my athletes — Leo, Joey, Mike — in her hands to see what she could do with them.

By the time Mother had decided, definitely and finally, on the seeds she would grow, I was one day away from being off the ventilator, my lungs were treated to a grudging compliment by Nurse Weaver ("I guess you'll do"), and my head was crammed with the names of different tomatoes: Mortgage Lifter, Amish Paste, Cherokee Purple, Early Red Chief, Principe Borghese, Zapotec Pleated, Arkansas Traveler, and Red House Free Standing, which, as the catalog copy informed us, was named after the Jimi Hendrix song. I wanted to tell Jay about that one. By the time Mother used the phone in my room to call up the catalogs and place her seed order, by the time Nurse Weaver removed the breathing tube and I tried out my hoarse, wispy voice, I thought the day might come when I could tell Jay things again, when I could tell him I loved him. I thought the day might come when I would be ready for spring.

We Are Giving Ourselves a Facial

My first time back at yoga, three months after what Officer Shane called "the incident," Gisela didn't say a word about my yellowing bruises and my baby-short hair, but she kept us in poses that brought blood to the face, "refreshing the brain," as she put it.

"When we *help* the heart bring blood to the head," she said, "we are giving it a *rest*. We think too *much* sometimes about *working* the heart, about running and jumping. The heart works for a *hundred* years without a rest, and we must *remember* it and thank it sometimes. We *must* say, 'Thank you, heart!'"

Thank you, heart, I thought to myself, traces of Gisela's accent flavoring my thought like a spice. I was still on vacation from Jay. I was planning to write him, for the first time in months, right after yoga.

"And when we do the *forward* bends," Gisela said, "when we let the blood *flow* to the head that way, we are giving ourselves a facial." That's when I knew she had changed the class just for me, that maybe she had planned to focus on back bends or hip stretches or who knows what, until she saw that I was in dire need of a facial. I loved her with the love of a thousand rabid football fans.

"Dear Faith," Jay had written back to me. "I understand completely. I'd like a vacation from me as well, but I don't have the choice, as you do."

"When we do these poses," Gisela said as we lifted our hipbones and lowered our heads into Downward-Facing Dog, "we are giving our bodies *information*. We arrange our bodies in these *lovely* ways and when we go back out into the world, they remember. And then the next time we feel anger or stress and we start to *round* the spine or hunch up the shoulders, we have this *nice* memory of the straight, elongated spine, of the *openness* of the backs of the knees, of the *length* of the neck, and these memories will help us walk through the world tall and proud."

"Maybe you want more than a vacation from me," he had written. "Maybe you need to be alone, Buddy, or with some other man. Whatever you need, Faith, I sure hope you find it. If it's what you want, I hope you will find a wonderful man, someone who will drink only of you, Faith, who will put his lips to the goblet of your body and drink as though he's dying of thirst. I had hoped to be that man for you, Buddy, and I'll be sorry for the rest of my life for what I'm not."

"Faith," Gisela said, "let us ask our hamstrings to release a *bit* more. If you ask them nicely, they *might* do it." I asked nicely and, without waiting for an answer, moved deeper into the pose.

I've got 306 days of sobriety, Buddy! Can you believe it?

"Good, Faith," Gisela said. "That's looking good. Now we relax into child's pose."

We all curled onto our mats in exhausted gratitude. Everyone was an expert at child's pose. I curled up so tightly that this thought could not find an entrance into my brain: *I don't want that man Jay was writing about. I want Jay.*

"This is a pose of rest and relaxation," Gisela said, her feet passing lightly by my ears. "Don't scrunch up as if you are working *hard* at something."

I must have worked hard at something, though, because after yoga I had barely enough energy to walk back to the dorm and crawl into bed. My brain worked just adequately enough for me to know that although I still loved Jay desperately, I did not have the energy to act on this love, even from afar. I didn't have the strength to write him a single postcard, to drive to Dayton and walk into the visitors' room and receive the two precious hugs he was allowed to give me. The fierce energy I'd had for him, the excess fuel that had driven me to volunteer my time all over the city, to read for the blind and to feed the elderly, the energy that had kept me up all night brainstorming term papers and learning foreign languages along with my students, cramming my brain with facts in hopes that my varied knowledge would cancel out the big, dumb mistake of my life — *that I had married an alcoholic and still harbored a ridiculous amount of love for him* — this energy had literally been punched out of me. Why couldn't the love have been punched out, too? If Richard had hit me maybe one more time, would the love have drained out of me as well as every ounce of my strength? Would I have been able to move away from the events of the past year the way we moved with great faith from one baseball season to the next, thinking this will be the year if only we can get a little more power in our lineup, if only we can find a good middle-relief man? If I could have accomplished the feat by hitting myself, I think I would have punched my still-fragile jaw with an unholy force.

In the middle of the day, right after yoga, when I should have been meeting with the stringent British lit professor who had repeatedly made it clear to me that she thought athletics had no place on a university campus, I fell into a deep and syrupy sleep, a clouded sleep from which I had no desire to wake. I dreamed that I marched right up to the lit professor and spat out the naked truth: that she, with her Ph.D. and her precious tenure and her published books on obscure British poets, that she was part of the life-support system for the Texas Longhorns football team and not the other way around. It was something I'd had to accept long ago.

That night, instead of going to the study lounge, I taped a sloppily written sign on my door that said COME IN IF YOU NEED ME. A few boys came in, clutching papers in their big hands, saying, "Miss Evers, you okay? Can you check out my thesis sentence?" I held out a hand for their papers; I approved of even the most pathetic thesis sentence. I curled up into child's pose and groaned my consent for whatever they asked. When Cam McClure came in to read me his short story, I forgot to be on the alert for photos, dreams, and Prague; I listened as if I were a little girl being treated to a bedtime story.

His story was his best of the year, or so it seemed to me in my delirium. It told about a young woman who, against her father's wishes, had her arm tattooed with a grinning skull. Her father beat her arm with a wire until the tattoo was ruined, until it was something other than what she had intended. This man's ability to change his daughter's body amazed me. The story was written in first-person, from the point of view of the girl's younger brother, who happened to be a high school football star and whose name happened to be Com. That had been Cam's assignment, to write a first-person story in a family setting. In the last line, the voice changed to address the sister: "Your skull healed up with the mouth slightly twisted, a little like your own cynical smile." Cam's teacher was the type who might take points off for this curve in the story's voice, who might write in the margin with a fat red marker *This is NOT first-person!* But I didn't want Cam to change the story. I didn't want to dissect his heartfelt effort with a discussion about point of view. So I reached out through the dim light of my room, patted his big, calloused hand, and said, "It's good, honey. I'm proud of you." I wanted to add that he was raking in the awards in the Game of Life, in my opinion, but I was far too tired.

Miss Evers, You Gotta Do Something

For weeks I tutored in my robe and nightgown, my hair a dirty fuzz. I didn't go even to the home games. I stopped enforcing study hours. I ceased visiting professors, sitting in on classes, meeting with the coaches. Coach Talwen slipped a note under my door that said, "Do you need a ride to the doctor?" I sent a note back to him, via an outfielder, that read "No."

I slept for a month, through the heart of baseball season and Lucy's first full pronunciation of my name on to my answering machine. I left my unanswered mail all over my bed so that it crunched when I turned over: clippings of Mother's column, letters from Jay, notes from Tonía written in pencil on wide-ruled notebook paper, and vitriolic letters from Richard, who had escaped a jail sentence but had been ordered to spend a thousand hours of his time designing and running the Web site for a battered women's shelter. My running shoes gathered dust under the bed. I slept through my team's wins and losses, with no idea of their record. I slept through countless academic traumas, through desperate phone calls from my staff and from Leo Rhodes's mother, a gynecologist, who suffered late-night panic attacks over the thought of her child graduating with a degree in sports management. The interesting thing, though, the thing that almost made me want to wake up, was that my team's grades didn't slip to the point of anyone being disqualified. Cory and Mike Winston, who had formed some strange alliance, helped me keep things going. They somehow found time, between classes and practice and games, between Cory's Longhorns for Christ meetings and the hours Mike spent watching televised stock-car races, to herd player after player into my room. They shoved figures into the darkness with a pleading, "He needs help with Russian lit, Miss Evers," or "Miss Evers, you gotta do something about this paper." They kept my old, peppy comments about the Game of Life on their lips. They sent a letter to Richard describing themselves as my personal bodyguards and warning him to stay away. Cory occasionally knelt by my bed and prayed out loud for me. He had let the shaved 7 on top of his skull grow in and had replaced it with a shaved cross. I stared down at it while he prayed for me, getting lost in the slick, shiny skin of his cross and the tiny wheatfields of hair that bordered it.

"Dear Lord," he said one morning, "our tutor, Miss Evers, she's having a hard time, Lord." Mike Winston sat in the background, his gaze steady on me over Cory's bowed head. "We don't know why You've sent her the trials that You have. We don't know why You gave her an alcoholic husband and allowed that man to commit murder with his vehicle. And we sure don't know why you allowed her body, Your temple, Lord, to suffer such physical harm."

"You're making your Lord sound like an asshole, Bell," Mike said. He had cut his eye patch of hair back so that both of his eyes were actually visible, pale blue and teasing.

"Shut up, Winston," Cory said. "Excuse me, Lord. But Lord, we know You have a reason for everything, and we trust in Your plan for us. We thank You for the lessons You bring us, and we know that a lot of those lessons are learned during the bad times. We ask, during this time, that You hold Miss Evers close to You, Lord, that You give her the strength to get through this time so she can try and get back on her feet, hopefully to do Your work."

"Cory," I said. "Sorry to interrupt. But that's try *to*. Try *to* get back on her feet. We don't ever say 'try and.' I know you hear it all over the place and you see it in the damn newspapers, but it's not correct. And do I have to go over 'hopefully' again?"

"I think your prayer's been answered, Bell," Mike said.

Cory grinned at me.

"What?" I said. I sat up a little straighter in bed, pulled another pillow behind me.

"That's the first time you've corrected me in so long," Cory said. "The other day we were saying 'hopefully' all over the place, just to see if you were in there, and you didn't say a word. I didn't know about 'try and,' though. Sorry about that."

"You misused 'hopefully' in front of me and I didn't say anything?"

"We both said it," Cory said. "The other night. You just looked at us like a zombie, Miss Evers."

I sat up completely, leaving my pillows behind, suddenly horrified by the idea of my entire team out there on the loose, abusing *hopefully* with impunity.

"Bring me my robe, Cory," I said. "I'm getting up."

Good News

Sometimes I think I'm like one of Mother's precious tomato seeds, that I had the strength in me all the time, ready to spring up with the right combination of light, soil, and water. The right mixture for me was all that sleep, Cory's bedside prayers to the god so colorfully portrayed on his T-shirt collection, Mike's presence and the memory of his lifting Richard off me, then those two tricking me out of bed with their awful grammar.

One of the first things I did in my new, wakeful life was go to a baseball game. I wore my most horrific burnt orange shirt, the one with white longhorn skulls stamped all over it in a dizzying pattern, and my burnt orange baseball cap with the big white *T* on the front. I pulled my hair through the hole in the cap into the tiniest ponytail imaginable; this made me feel young and cute, capable of standing up on the bleachers and screaming rhyming slogans at my players. When Cory Bell hit a double, I jumped up and down on the bleachers until they rattled. I screamed myself hoarse after that, yelling for pop flies as well as base hits. Coach sent over one of the ball boys, a high-schooler whose face was sandy with acne, to ask me if I was all right.

"Tell him I'm great," I said. "Never better."

"Winston wants to know if you need anything. Coke or a hot dog or somethin'. Told me to get you somethin' if you want it."

"Tell Mike to hit one out for me," I said.

The boy turned away with a roll of the eyes, obviously not looking forward to delivering my corny message to Michael.

As I watched Mike swing his weighted bat in the on-deck circle, as I watched him slide the weights off and step up to the plate, the newly light bat small against his huge shoulder, I thought, *Screw answering the Mistress's question.* I thought, *Let's see you knock the shit out of that ball, Michael Winston.*

It was a deep blue spring day, one of the days that make our seventh-circle-of-hell summers absolutely worth it. It was warm enough to think about swimming, picnics, obscenely ripe tomatoes. Warm enough that when Mike whacked a high fastball with the fat torso of the bat, it almost sailed over the fence. It rose, and rose, and the infielders stood frozen as the center fielder raced back, and the slightest breeze or sigh of fate would have taken it over. It hit the edge of the fence and bounced back in and rattled around between the center fielder's feet until Mike had an easy triple that brought home Cory and Pete and put our team ahead. It was every bit as good as a home run, and I used the last of my voice yelling over it.

That day seems like years ago, now that we've gone through another summer and another football season and we're back to the start of baseball, now that Mike is playing for the Orioles' farm team up in Rochester, New York, and Cory has graduated and gone off to India to preach the gospel, or, as he calls it, "the Good News." He sends me post-cards sometimes, addressed to "Miss Evers," with Bible verses crammed into any available space. Mike sends me cards with reports of his batting average and complaints about the dreary weather up in Rochester. Occasionally, he has news of Micah, who has married and now has a wife and a baby boy to help him spend his millions.

I write to them sometimes about things I've learned, things I've learned sitting in on classes with my new ball-players or from just sitting in on my life. I tell them it feels good to try to be good to people, no matter how bad they are to you, that being kind feels better in the end than being cruel and lazy and vengeful, and as I'm writing these things to them I know they sound basic, I know it sounds like I'm saying, "Mike, the sky is blue," but we have to learn this stuff some time. At some point our mothers had to take us in their arms and hold us up and point to the sky and say, "Look at the sky, honey. It's blue."

Mike and Cory write me back not at the dorms but at my new house in South Austin, which I bought with the raise I negotiated when they fired Coach Walston and brought in the new coaching staff for football, and with some help from Mother, who made a bundle selling her special hybrid seed from Almost the World's Largest Tomato to one of the big seed companies.

It's a wonderful house. It's shaded by a live oak in back that brings me hours of entertainment; I stretch out on the ground and hear Gisela's voice saying, "Feel the support of the earth beneath you," and I look up into the tree's compli-cated curves and the designs of its leaves. I have a garden, which Mother helps me with when she comes to visit. She gives me more advice than a person with only two ears could possibly take in, but I grab on to what I can and she's happy to repeat the rest. She's taught me how to coax a seed from the ground, how to bring it along to a size where it can stand up to the Texas sun. It takes some faith to believe that a tiny seed can grow into a tomato plant taller than me and heavy with tomatoes, but I water and fertilize and pinch off the suckers like it's my religion. I like my garden best when Lucy comes over and squats down to pat the soft curls of lettuce, then looks up at me and says with incredible articulation and wisdom, "Lettuce."

Sometimes when I'm out in the yard, thinning the lettuce or admiring the live oak, I catch a glimpse of my reflection in the big bay window of my back room. I'm just a small part of the reflection; it's filled up with my tree, the sky, and slick, white streaks of sun. My face, though it's just a blur in the window, is different from the one I had. There's a slight unevenness around my jaw; my nose is not as sharp. Mother says, "Nonsense, Sugar, you're just as darling as ever," but I know my face has the look of something that was broken and has healed. I don't mind it. I don't think it's *darling*, but it has the beauty of something that's well worn, something that has been distressed to the point of softness and grace.

And Jay. Jay got bumped out of rehab jail six months early because they needed the space for newer offenders; he was transferred to a halfway house in East Austin. He has some free time, on the weekends in between his multiple stay-sober meetings and his "humility job," which is so humiliating he won't even tell me what it is, and what we have come to after all this is dates. We go on dates. Jay calls me up on the halfway house pay phone and asks if I am free at a certain time, and if I am we make very specific plans, such as dinner and a movie or an excursion to an art gallery where we walk around and look at the paintings and sometimes say, "Lucy could have done that one." I nervously choose something to wear and make sure my hair is at its shiniest and Jay picks me up in a taxi, his license having been suspended for obvious reasons. We say stiff, funny things to each other like, "You look very nice tonight."

"So do you."

"Thank you."

At the end of our dates we kiss good night on my front porch, and occasionally Jay lapses back into his old self and says, "When you gonna let me get to second base, Buddy?"

"Sometime," I say.

Then we smile stretched, wild, laden smiles at each other and I back in the screen door and close the real door and throw the deadbolt, more to give myself an obstacle to getting back out than to keep Jay from getting in. I wait for the sound of the cab driving away, then I smear my hands all over myself and call out Jay's name like a cheer.

Sometimes, because it makes Jay very happy, I go to the five-thirty family meeting at his halfway house and sit with the other wives while they chain-smoke and tell their sordid stories. They've been beaten, dragged around by their hair, they've seen their children go hungry while their husbands guzzled up the grocery money. I never say a word. There's never a part where my story seems to fit in, although it certainly has its sordid aspects. Sometimes I consider telling something about Jay, about how he and his counselor burned his black spiral notebook as a symbol that his old life is over, or about how he has hard days still, days when he clutches his head and wants to drink or get high so badly that he almost cries with rage when the halfway house counselors offer him something normal: a glass of water, a bowl of soup. I've considered sharing what he told me about how he paces the floor all night, or stands downstairs at midnight in his boxers, the halfway house pay phone squeezed up between his shoulder and his ear, telling his AA sponsor he doesn't know if he can make it, he feels like he's going fucking crazy, and if he's sober for like five years then can he just be a normal guy, a guy who has a beer sometimes after work, who takes a hit off a joint at a party? Jay knows the answers to those questions, but he seems to need to ask them over and over. He needs to hear Roots, his dreadlocked sponsor who still manages to cultivate a semi-stoned aura, say, "Five years, shit. You worry about today, Jaybird."

Sometimes I feel the old loneliness scraping at me from all those nights of trying to love on Jay's passed-out self, from having to wash my scent from his face so he wouldn't know that he'd inadvertently given me a few seconds of pleasure, and I think about speaking it to the other women. But somehow I'm not ready to talk to them. I'm not ready to trot my naked masturbating self out on that table covered in chewed-up Styrofoam coffee cups and overflowing ashtrays. Sometimes I bum a cigarette from one of them, usually Dolores, and I just hold it, letting it burn down to the filter, so that until I find the space to speak up, to ask them if they go on dates with their husbands too, they can see that we have something in common.

I have a date with Jay tonight, in fact. And a new black dress to wear. The dress is short enough to show off my brand-new calf muscles; I've been running a few wind sprints with my boys. In between flashing my legs and flirting and listening to Jay's new language, the one that never equates beer with food, I'll tell him about this year's team, about how promising they are, about our hopes for a championship. I think this should be a good season. I think we have a chance.